LEONARDO'S JUDAS

LEONARDO'S JUDAS

❦

Leo Perutz

*Translated from the German
by Eric Mosbacher*

Arcade Publishing • New York
LITTLE, BROWN AND COMPANY

COPYRIGHT © 1988 BY PAUL ZSOLNAY VERLAG G.M.B.H., VIENNA, DARMSTADT
TRANSLATION COPYRIGHT © 1989 BY WILLIAM COLLINS SONS & CO. LTD.

ALL RIGHTS RESERVED. NO PART OF THIS BOOK MAY BE REPRODUCED
IN ANY FORM OR BY ANY ELECTRONIC OR MECHANICAL MEANS,
INCLUDING INFORMATION STORAGE AND RETRIEVAL SYSTEMS,
WITHOUT PERMISSION IN WRITING FROM THE PUBLISHER, EXCEPT
BY A REVIEWER WHO MAY QUOTE BRIEF PASSAGES IN A REVIEW.

FIRST U.S. EDITION

The characters and events in this book are fictitious.
Any similarity to real persons, living or dead,
is coincidental and not intended by the author.

Library of Congress Catalog Card Number 89-80614

ISBN: 1-55970-002-5

HC

Published in the United States by Arcade Publishing, Inc., New York,
a Little, Brown company.

*Published simultaneously in Canada
by Little, Brown & Company (Canada) Limited*

PRINTED IN THE UNITED STATES OF AMERICA

Note

This is Perutz's last book. After his death at Ischl on 25 August 1957 I was asked to look through the completed manuscript and prepare it for the press. I undertook the task the more gladly and the more respectfully as I always regarded Perutz as my especially admired teacher.

ALEXANDER LERNET-HOLENIA

Chapter 1

On a blustery day in March 1498, when showers of rain on the Lombard plain were interrupted every now and again by belated snow flurries, the prior of the Dominican monastery of Santa Maria delle Grazie went to the castle in Milan to wait upon Duke Ludovico Maria Sforza, commonly known as Il Moro, the Moor, to seek his support in a matter that had been troubling him for some considerable time.

The duke was by this time no longer the statesman and strategist of calculated boldness and swift action who had so often succeeded in keeping war from his territory by sowing unrest in that of all his neighbours, thus deflecting hostile forces from his frontiers and increasing his power. His good fortune and his reputation were declining and, as he used to say himself, an ounce of good fortune is sometimes worth more than ten pounds of wisdom. The time had passed when he called Pope Alexander VI his chaplain, the King of France his always available courier, the Republic of Venice – the so-called Serenissima – his heavily laden pack-ass, and the Holy Roman Emperor his best *condottiere*. The French king in question, Charles VIII, was dead, and his successor, Louis XII, as the grandson of a Visconti, laid claim to the dukedom of Milan himself. Maximilian, the Holy Roman Emperor, was tied up in so many complicated affairs that he himself was in need of help. As for the Serenissima, she had turned out to be such a restive neighbour that Il Moro had given her to understand that he would, if he chose, join the league of her enemies, deny her a foot of dry land on which to grow corn, and send her fishing far out in the open sea. For he still had several tons of gold which would enable him to make war if the necessity arose.

Il Moro received the prior of Santa Maria delle Grazie in his castle in the Hall of the Gods and Giants, which owed its name to the frescos that covered two of its walls; on the third, a *Vision of Ezekiel*, dating from the days of the Visconti, was just discernible in spite of the faded and partly peeling paint. It was here that the duke used to attend to state business in the morning, and he was seldom to be found there alone, for at that time of day he liked having familiar faces present or within calling distance. Being alone, even for a few minutes, oppressed him and made him feel uneasy, as if he had been abandoned by everyone, and a sense of grim foreboding reduced the widest space to a prison cell in his mind.

On that day at that moment, then, the privy councillor Simone di Treio had just finished reporting to the duke on the steps that would have to be taken to receive the High Steward of the Kingdom of Naples, who was expected at court. Also present was a secretary of the ducal chancery, who was taking notes. The treasurer Landriano and the military commander da Corte, who was already said to prefer French gold crowns to any other currency, were standing in a window recess casting an expert eye over two horses, a Barbary and a big Neapolitan, which were being led backwards and forwards by grooms in the old courtyard below, while the duke's equerry discussed the price with their owner, a German horse-dealer, who was to be seen continually shaking his head.

In the hall, close to the open fire and beneath a fearsome giant painted on the wall who puffed out his cheeks in a most alarming manner, sat the lady Lucrezia Crivelli, who was credited with being the duke's mistress. With her were two gentlemen: the court poet Bellincioli, a gaunt man with the melancholy expression of a monkey afflicted with angina, and the lyre player, Migliorotti, who was known at court as the Fennel. For just as sweets and other titbits made with fennel are served only at the end of a meal, when everyone has satisfied his appetite, so did the duke generally send for him only when he was replete with all other kinds of entertainment. This Fennel was a taciturn individual, and when he did say something it generally sounded dull and commonplace; besides, he had a croaking voice and therefore preferred to keep his mouth shut. But he had the gift of expressing his thoughts and feelings with skill and clarity through his lyre, and now, while Il Moro warmly welcomed the prior and led him to an armchair, he played with devout solemnity, as if it were a hymn in church, the tune of a Milanese popular song that began with the words:

> Thieves and robbers prowl at night,
> Good people, hold your purses tight.

For it was known at court that the prior on principle never missed an opportunity to take advantage of the duke's generosity; he generally introduced his plea for a subsidy by complaining that the bad weather had held back the vines at the monastery's two estates, and this had plunged (or was about to plunge) him into grave financial difficulties.

The duke's mistress, who had risen from her chair by the fire and was approaching the prior, turned her head and cast a glance of severe disapproval at the Fennel. Her upbringing had been pious and, though she no longer regarded every priest or monk as God's personal representative on earth, she still considered that money given to the Church was money well spent, from which the greatest benefits could be expected to flow.

Meanwhile the prior had sunk into an armchair with a slight grunt. In reply to the duke's inquiry about his health, he said he had been suffering for weeks from loss of appetite, and he called God to witness that for two days he had been unable to eat anything but a little bread and half a partridge wing. If this went on, he added, he would soon have no strength left.

Surprisingly he turned out not to have come to appeal for money this time, for he made no mention of the vines, which must certainly have failed to set this year too. Instead, without any preamble, he started talking about what he considered to be the cause of the deplorable state of his health.

"It's that Christ with His apostles," he said, fanning himself. "That is, if it really is a Christ, for, apart from a few arms and legs, you can't make out anything at all, and I can't tell to which of the apostles they belong. I've had enough of it. That man's going too far. For months you never see him at all and, when he does put in an appearance, he spends half the day staring at the painting without even picking up a brush. Believe me, he started this picture only in order to worry me to death."

The Fennel had accompanied the whole of this speech with another tune. This time it was that of a derisive song that the Milan populace sang when they had had enough of a bad, long-winded and boring sermon and wanted no more of it. The words were:

> You've bored us stiff, and that will do,
> We're walking out, farewell, adieu.

"Reverend father," said the duke, "you have entered a smithy's forge – here I'm continually caught between the hammer and the anvil. A day seldom passes without a similar or entirely different complaint being made about this man. Now, as everyone knows, I am as devoted to him as to a brother, and I shall never cease to love him. In many of his arts he seems to be in the doldrums, and since he began applying himself to experiments and mathematics – whether out of defiance or out of genuine enthusiasm I don't know – he can't be counted on for so much as a little madonna. That, he says, is a task for Salai, his apprentice, who until last year used to mix his paints."

"I believe that at the moment he's more preoccupied than ever with the problems of painting," said the poet Bellincioli. "He talked to me only yesterday, with that peculiar intensity of his, about the ten high offices that the painter's eye must be responsible for: light and shade, outline and colour, figure and background, distance and proximity, movement and rest. He also assured me quite seriously that painting must be regarded as superior to the art of the physician, for it could resurrect those long dead and enable the living to forswear death. A man who despairs of his art does not talk like that."

"He has become a dreamer and a teller of fairy tales," said the military commander da Corte, briefly turning his attention away from the two horses down in the courtyard. "His portable bridge for streams with high or low banks – I don't think I shall ever see it, except on paper. He aims high, but leaves everything unfinished."

"What you, my gracious lord, are pleased to call the doldrums may perhaps arise from his fear of making mistakes," the treasurer Landriano said, turning to the duke, "and his fear may increase from year to year as his knowledge increases and his skill matures. Perhaps he should forget a little of his art and his knowledge if he is to do fine work again."

"That may be," said the prior, looking bored. "But the chief thing he should bear in mind is that a refectory is a place for sitting and eating in, not for atoning for one's sins. I can't stand any longer the sight of the trestles and the swing bridge and the wall behind them just brushed over, and still less can I stand the perpetual smell of plaster and linseed oil, varnish and paint to which I'm continually subjected. And when he sets fire to damp wood six times a day, producing smoke thick enough to make our eyes smart, merely, as he explains, to make sure what colour the smoke is when seen from a distance . . . what I should like to know is what all this has to do with the Last Supper."

"We have now heard three or four different views about this fallow period in Messer Leonardo's work, and it is only fair that we should let him speak for himself. He is here in this building now. But let me advise you, reverend father, to deal gently with him, for pressure will get you nowhere."

With this, he sent for Leonardo.

The secretary found the master bareheaded in the rain, crouching over his sketch-book, in which he had caught the movements of the big Neapolitan horse and the proportions of its outstretched hind leg. When he heard why he was wanted and that the prior of Santa Maria delle Grazie was there, he closed his sketch-book and silently followed the secretary across the courtyard and up the steps, deep in thought. Outside the door of the hall he stopped to add a few strokes to the sketch of the horse's leg. Then he went in, still so absorbed in his thoughts that he made to greet the Fennel before paying his respects to the duke and the prior; at first he seemed not to notice the others present.

"Messer Leonardo, you are the occasion of the very welcome visit with which the reverend father has surprised us so early in the day," the duke said, and those who knew him and his ways could conclude from these words that the implied rebuke was directed not so much at Leonardo as at the prior. For Il Moro disliked surprises, and he was never glad to see an unexpected visitor.

"I came here in spite of the bad weather, which is really not good for my health, Messer Leonardo," the prior began, "so that you might give me an explanation in the presence of His Most Serene Highness, who is the patron of our monastery. For it is the Holy Church that through me has given you the opportunity to show your skill, and you promised me that with God's help you would produce a work that would have no equal in the whole of Lombardy. Moreover I can produce not one or two but hundreds of witnesses to your promise. Now months have again passed without your having done any work on the picture, and so far you've made no real progress with it at all."

"You surprise me, Father," Leonardo replied. "I am working so hard on this *Last Supper* that I quite forget to eat or sleep."

"How dare you say that to me?" exclaimed the prior, flushing with anger. "To me, who visit that refectory three times a day and, if by any chance you're there at all for once, see you just gazing into space. Is that what you call work? Am I an ox to be led by the nose?"

Messer Leonardo, undeterred by this outburst, went on: "I have been working on it in my head so tirelessly that I should soon be able to satisfy you, and be in a position to show those who come after me what I can do, but for the fact that I am still searching for one thing, that is, the head of the apostle who . . ."

"You and your apostle's head," the prior interrupted angrily. "On the south wall opposite Montorfano has long since finished his *Crucifixion*, which also has several apostles in it, though he began it less than a year ago."

At the mention of Montorfano, a painter who, in his Milanese colleagues' opinion, did little credit to the city, the Fennel played some ear-splitting discords on his lyre, while the privy councillor di Treio stepped forward and said politely if somewhat hesitantly that the reverend gentleman must forgive him, but Montorfanos could be found by the dozen at every street corner.

"He makes a living by daubing walls," the poet Bellincioli said, with a shrug. "The boys who mix his colours split their sides with laughter at his *Crucifixion*."

"*I* regard it as a very competent piece of work," said the prior who, when he had once formed an opinion, stuck to it obstinately. "And at all events it's finished. What I most appreciate in Montorfano is his ability to give the surface of his pictures the appearance of a noble figure standing out from the background, and that is what he has done in this case."

"Except that he painted a bag of nuts instead of the Saviour on the cross," remarked Bellincioli.

"And what do you think of that *Crucifixion*, Messer Leonardo?" asked the duke's mistress, who hoped to embarrass the master of so many arts. For he disliked expressing opinions about the works of other artists, particularly those about whom he could find nothing good to say. As she expected, he tried to evade the question, which he found particularly inopportune in the prior's presence.

"You, madam, are certainly a better judge of that," he said with a defensive gesture and a smile.

The duke was amused and curious. "Oh no, we shan't let you get away with that," he said; "we want your real opinion."

"I often think," Messer Leonardo said after a few moments'

consideration, "that painting is bound to deteriorate from one generation to the next if painters merely copy existing paintings instead of learning from nature and applying what they learn . . ."

The prior interrupted him.

"Come to the point," he said. "What we want to know is what you think of that *Crucifixion*."

"It's a very pious work," Messer Leonardo now said, weighing his words carefully; "and whenever I see it I feel all the suffering of the martyred Saviour."

Some happy phrases that could be interpreted as a peal of merry laughter came from the Fennel's lyre.

"It is so true to life," Leonardo continued. "Another thing I have to say about Giovanni Montorfano is that he possesses a masterly skill for dissecting a hare or a pheasant which in itself is evidence enough of his manual dexterity."

The notes of the lyre frisked and gambolled, and the prior's angry voice made itself heard above the general tittering.

"We know, everyone knows, Messer Leonardo, that you have the wickedest tongue in Milan," he said, "and those who have dealings with you always land in trouble and suffer harm. The good friars of San Donato have been complaining about you for years. I wish I had listened to them."

Messer Leonardo did not lose his composure. "You are referring," he said, "to the *Adoration of the Shepherds* I began painting for the friars of San Donato and never finished because Lorenzo the Magnificent stepped in to support me."

"I don't know whether it was an *Adoration* or what Lorenzo the Magnificent had to do with it," the prior replied. "All I know is that the friars were the losers. But it is evident from what you said yourself that you were paid twice for the work, first by the friars and then by Lorenzo the Magnificent, and both lost as a result."

"It seems to me that there must be a story behind what Messer Leonardo has been telling us," said the duke. "If there isn't, it means I don't know my Leonardo. Isn't that so, Leonardo? Then let us hear it."

"There is a story, though it's not a very amusing one," Leonardo replied, "and if in spite of that you wish to hear it, my lord, I must begin with the fact, as the reverend prior has just reminded me, that fourteen years ago in Florence I made an agreement with the friars of San Donato. I promised them . . ."

"You were always a great one for promises," the prior interrupted.

"I promised to paint an *Adoration of the Shepherds* for their high altar; on the same day they gave me a pail of red wine as my first payment, and I set to work. I soon realized that the shepherds and kings would be no problem. I proposed to give one of them Lorenzo's features. To me it seemed that a far more important part of my task was to show people at large receiving the message of salvation: to show the tidings being brought to artisans, town councillors, peasants, barrow-women, barbers, coachmen, porters, road sweepers, to depict them in taverns, courtyards, streets, and wherever people forgather, and someone comes hurrying along with the news – and it is even shouted into the ear of a deaf man, the news that the Saviour has been born that night."

The Fennel accompanied these last words with a tune that was as simple and pious as the songs sung by mountain peasants when making their way along snow-covered roads to Mass on Christmas Eve. And Messer Leonardo fell silent and listened while the tune went on, to end in a swell of jubilation. He stood and listened until it ended with the last quiet surge of joy. Then he went on:

"It struck me in connection with that deaf man, who was to hear the tidings of salvation like everyone else, that it was very important to observe and follow his changes of expression, and to note how his weary indifference to everything that does not concern him gives way to a restlessness for which at first he cannot account, then to the agony of not being able to understand, and then to the fear that something has happened that might have bad consequences for him. But then comes the moment when he senses rather than understands that salvation has come for him too. The happy excitement of this is not yet reflected in his face, which at first shows only impatience, because now he wants to find out all about it quickly. But to capture all this with my pencil in my sketch-book I needed to associate for some time with a deaf person, and I couldn't find one . . ."

Da Corte's voice interrupted from the window.

"So that's settled at last," he said. "They've actually come to terms. The German has nodded."

"No, it's not settled, not by a long chalk," Landriano objected. "Look, the equerry's still remonstrating with him. These Germans are as tough as leather in money matters. You can't get them to budge, it's easier to bargain with a Jew."

Silence returned. The two gentlemen went on watching the horse-trading, while the sound of quiet, regular breathing came from the prior's armchair. A boyish-looking servant had come in with a bowl of fruit and was about to slip out again as noiselessly as he had entered when the duke's mistress beckoned to him and told him in a whisper to attend to the fire, which was dying down.

"I couldn't find a deaf person in Florence," Leonardo went on. "There didn't seem to be a single person in the city who was deaf enough for my purpose. I went to the markets day after day and talked to the buyers and the sellers, I sent my servant to neighbouring villages, and when he came back in the evening he told me about blind men and lame men and cripples of all sorts, but he had not come across a single deaf person. But one day when I came back from market I found a man waiting for me in my house, and he was stone deaf. He was an exile who had returned surreptitiously to Florence and he was picked up by Lorenzo's henchmen when wandering about the streets. To punish him, and to do me a favour (so he thought), Lorenzo had him deprived of his hearing. Just imagine it, gentlemen. A crude hand had smashed the sensitive instrument, placed by the Supreme Intelligence in such a confined space to receive the innumerable sounds of the world and repeat them faithfully, of whatever nature they might be, and that had been done for my benefit. You will appreciate,

gentlemen, that I could not go on working on that picture, and did not want to stay another day in a city in which a favour of that sort had been done me. It is true that the friars of San Donato had wasted a pail of wine, as well as the money they paid me for paints, oil and white lead. But how little does their loss weigh in comparison with that suffered by the exile because of that dreadful *Adoration* by kings who acknowledge God but have no respect for His marvellous works."

In the quiet that prevailed in the hall the prior's breathing was now distinctly audible. He had fallen asleep in his armchair, exhausted by the drive on bad roads and by argument and counter-argument, and because he was quickly tired by any story that he could not avoid listening to. Sleep had smoothed and removed the hardness from his features, and his face, with sparse strands of white hair falling over his brow, was that of a very peaceable old gentleman, remote from worldly affairs; and thus, while fast asleep, he conducted his case against Messer Leonardo more effectively than he had done previously with taunts and angry outbursts.

The duke broke the brief silence.

"Messer Leonardo," he said, "you have made us see in our mind's eye with great clarity the wonderful *Adoration* that you planned, and it is deplorable that all the trouble you took over it led to nothing but the little story you have told us. It was a sad story but, as you told it, it was good to listen to. But you have still not told us why you so obstinately refrain from working on the *Last Supper*, when the old gentleman there is pressing you for its completion with an urgency that can derive only from a great love for you and your art."

"It is because I do not yet have and have not yet seen the most important thing of all, Judas's face," Leonardo replied. "Please understand me, gentlemen, it is not any ordinary rogue or villain I seek; I need the wickedest man in the whole of Milan, he's the one I'm after, so that I may give Judas his features. I search for him everywhere, wherever I am, day and night, in the streets, the taverns, the markets and even, Your Serene Highness, at your court; and until I find him I cannot go on with the work – unless I paint Judas with his back to the viewer, but that would bring me dishonour. Find me my Judas, Your Serene Highness, and you'll see how I work."

Di Treio, the privy councillor, quietly interrupted. "Did you not mention recently," he said respectfully, "that you had found the wickedest person in Milan in the person of a Florentine of an old family who, you said, though a rich man, made his daughter spin wool until late at night and didn't give her enough to eat? I met her recently in the market, where she was trying to sell one of her few dresses to raise some money."

"I was mistaken about that man, who conducts his usurious business here under the name of Bernardo Boccetta," Messer Leonardo said with something like regret in his voice. "He's nothing but a contemptible miser. Rather than keep a cat, he uses a stick to chase the mice in his house. He would have pocketed the thirty pieces of silver and not betrayed Christ. No, Judas's sin was not avarice, and it was not for the sake of money that he kissed Our Lord in the garden of Gethsemane."

"He did it because of the envy and malice in his heart, both of which exceeded all human proportion," said Bellincioli.

"No," said Messer Leonardo, "for the Saviour would have forgiven him envy and malice, both of which are innate in human beings. Where has there ever been a great man who has not been touched by the envy and malice of lesser men? And that is how I shall portray the Redeemer in this *Last Supper*; burning with the desire to expiate all the world's sins, including envy and malice, by His sacrificial death. But the sin of Judas he did not forgive."

"Because Judas knew good and yet followed evil?"

"No," said Messer Leonardo, "for who can live in the world and pursue his calling without sometimes practising treachery and doing evil?"

At that moment, before the duke found an answer to these bold words, the equerry appeared in the doorway, and it was evident from his expression that he had completed the deal with the German horse-dealer. The duke gave orders to inspect the two horses which were now his, and the whole company followed him downstairs.

So it came about that, apart from the prior asleep in his chair and the servant poking the fire, Messer Leonardo found himself suddenly alone in the great Hall of the Gods and Giants. As if he had been waiting for this moment, he produced his sketch-book from under his belt and, as he recalled the prior's posture and expression while scolding him, he wrote down the following sentences from right to left, that is, in mirror writing, on a page only partially covered with sketches: "The apostle Peter, angry: make him raise his left arm, his fingers bent at shoulder height. Make his brow low and contracted, his teeth clenched and a curve at the corners of his mouth. Like that it will be right. Make his neck wrinkled."

He put the sketch-book back under his belt, and when he looked up his eyes fell on the servant, a boy of not more than seventeen who was standing in front of the fire holding a log and gazing at him with a tense expression, at once excited and hesitant. Leonardo beckoned to him to approach.

"You look," he said, "as if you had something to say to me and were going to choke if I didn't let you."

The boy nodded and took a deep breath.

"I know I have no right to approach you here," he said, "and so far I have not had an opportunity to do the slightest thing for you. But seeing that that Boccetta was mentioned here just now . . ."

"What's your name, young man?"

"Girolamo, but here they call me Giamino. I'm the son of Ceppo, the gold brocade weaver, you knew him. His workshop was next door to the barber's in the fish-market, and it's still there, and I saw you at his house two or three times."

"Is he dead?"

"Yes," said the boy, glancing at the log he was still holding. After a short pause he continued: "He killed himself, may God have mercy on his soul. He was ill and dogged by misfortune. Last of all he was cheated of the little he had left by the man you've been talking about, Boccetta. You said he was only a miser but, believe me, he's also a swindler, and a shameless one at that. I could tell you other things about him too – so many, the fire would have gone out before I finished. But no, he's not a Judas. How could he be a Judas, for there's not a soul in the world whom he loves."

"You know Judas's secret? You know what his sin was? You know why he betrayed Christ?'

"He betrayed Him when he realized he loved Him," the boy replied. "He could see that he was going to love Him too much, and his pride would not permit that."

"Yes, that was the sin of Judas, it was pride that made him betray his love."

Leonardo searched the boy's face as he said this, as if he were looking for something that might be worth capturing in a picture. Then he took the log from him and examined it.

"This is ash," he decided. "Good wood, but it gives only a moderate heat. Pine's just the same. The flames should be fed with oak logs, they produce a proper glowing heat."

This disconcerted the lad, who was still thinking about Judas.

"Are you talking about the fires of hell?" he asked. He would not have been very surprised to hear that Messer Leonardo, a master of every art and discipline, who had even devised a self-turning spit for the ducal kitchens, had decided to introduce improvements into the furnishings of hell.

"No, I'm talking about the furnace I've built," said Messer Leonardo, turning to leave.

The German horse-dealer was still down below in the old courtyard. He had a leather purse in his hand, for he had been paid only partly in bills of exchange and had been given eighty ducats in cash. He was an unusually handsome man of about forty, tall, with lively eyes and a dark beard, which he wore trimmed in the Levantine fashion. He was in a good mood, pleased with the world as he found it, for he had obtained the price he wanted for the two horses.

When he saw a man of commanding, almost intimidating, presence crossing the courtyard towards him, his first thought was that the duke had sent him – perhaps something was wrong with the horses. But he soon realized that the man was sunk in thought and had no specific purpose in mind, so he stepped aside to make way for him. As he did so he was trying to force the purse into his coat pocket; he tilted his head back a little with a look of curious enquiry on his face, as if he were looking for conversation and ready, perhaps, to strike up an acquaintanceship.

But Messer Leonardo, whose mind was on the Judas in his *Last Supper,* had no eyes for him.

Chapter 2

The horse-dealer who had had such a fleeting encounter with the Florentine Messer Leonardo in the courtyard of the ducal castle was called Joachim Behaim. He was born in Bohemia, which was still his home, but he preferred being known as a German, which gained him more respect and prestige in the countries through which he travelled. He had come to Milan from the Levant to sell his horses, which were exceptionally fine specimens and of such outstanding pedigree that he considered that the only appropriate place for them was in a ducal stud. Had he failed to come to terms with Il Moro's equerry he would have had to try his luck at the courts of Mantua, Ferrara or Urbino. Now that he had sold the two horses, whose grooming and maintenance cost him a tidy sum every day, and had got his price for them, he could have gone back to Venice, where business awaited him. For he dealt in everything that could be bought at favourable prices in the countries of the Levant, and in the warehouses of Venice he had cloth and blankets of the finest quality wool and Cypriot silk gauze to the value of more than eight hundred sequins. The fluctuations in price of these and other products of the Levant needed his constant attention if he were not to miss the right moment to market his goods.

But he could not make up his mind to leave Milan. Not that life in that city appealed to him particularly. True, at that time it had attracted the best artists and scholars in Italy to its houses and palaces, and everyone from duke to cobbler wrote, rhymed, criticized, painted, sang, played the fiddle or the lyre or, if incapable of any of these things, merely interpreted Dante.

Joachim Behaim rated this world-famous city no more highly than any other, for he felt at home wherever he could buy or sell advantageously and drink his two measures of good Cyprus wine or hippocras in entertaining company in the evening without anyone getting the better of him. The only reason he stayed on in Milan was that a day or two before he had set eyes on a girl whose looks, whose carriage, whose eyes when they met his, whose smile, had robbed him of his peace and so captivated him that he could not stop thinking about her day or night. Like all lovers, he was convinced that never would he see a lovelier or more attractive girl even if he scoured the world for her.

It would have been inconsistent with his obstinate nature to have admitted to himself that he had succumbed to an infatuation of this kind and that it was his desire to see the girl again and get to know her that kept him in Milan. The girls and women he had previously met at home or abroad had never been anything but dispensers of brief pleasures, creatures with whom to spend an enjoyable hour. He had felt love for none of them, and he refused to admit that this time he had really fallen in love. He kept assuring himself that it was not for this girl's sake that he was staying on in Milan; such an idea was ridiculous, and nobody who knew him would believe it for a moment. One girl was as good as another, after all. The fact was he had been intending for ages to collect a long-outstanding debt due to him in this city, and after so many years of pressing for repayment and vainly waiting for it, he was surely not going to waste this opportunity to lay a hand on his money at last. No one could expect him simply to abandon a claim that was cut and dried, he was not that sort of person, right was right and always would be. All this he went on repeating to himself for so long that he ended by convincing himself that this was the real reason why he was staying on in Milan.

As for the young lady who all unsuspecting had so thoroughly undermined his peace, he had seen her in the Via San Jacopo, which leads past the fruit and vegetable market, at the time when the Angelus is rung, that is, when it was more crowded than usual, with people flocking to the market to buy cabbages, turnips, apples, figs or olives and mingling with worshippers coming from church. He might well have passed without noticing her, particularly as she kept her eyes downcast, as good manners prescribed, and he was thinking about the horses he had for sale. But then he heard a song being sung over in the market place, and he turned and, in the midst of the noise and bustle, the baskets of grapes, the barrows piled with vegetables, the braying donkeys, the swearing porters, the squabbling peasants, the haggling women and the prowling cats, he saw a man standing on a vegetable barrel and singing in a melodious voice, as unperturbed as if he were alone in the market place and all round him was quiet. The man made the motion of plucking the strings of a lyre, which made Joachim Behaim laugh, until he noticed that this strange singer was looking expectantly in his, Behaim's, direction; and when he turned to look at him he noticed the girl.

It was immediately obvious to him that the man's song was directed at her. She had stopped and was smiling, and it was a smile of a special kind; there were all sorts of things in it: recognition and a greeting, embarrassment and pleasure, amusement and something like gratitude. With a barely perceptible movement of her head she nodded at the singer on the barrel. Then she turned, still smiling, and her eyes lit upon Joachim Behaim, standing there as if in a trance, his eyes confessing to a newly kindled passion. She looked at him, and the smile still lingering on her face became a different smile and was now directed at him.

They looked at each other. Their lips were closed, the expression on their faces was that of persons who are strangers to each other, but their eyes asked questions: Who are you? Where are you from? Where are you going? Will you love me?

Then her eyes freed themselves from his as one frees oneself from an embrace; she gave him a scarcely perceptible nod, and was gone.

Joachim Behaim awoke as from a spell and hurried after her;

he did not want to lose sight of her, he went as fast as he could, with a great deal of cursing and swearing because, as always when he was in a hurry, every porter and mule driver got in his way. And as he hurried after her like this he noticed a handkerchief lying in the street in front of him. He picked it up and ran it through his fingers, for he knew everything about fabrics of all kinds, whether they were linen or silk, whether they came from Flanders, Florence or the Levant; and he scarcely needed to glance at the handkerchief in his hand to recognize it for the finest woven linen with a silky sheen known in the trade as *boccaccino* – it was worn by the women and girls of Milan who pinned it to the side of their dress as fashion required. Had he been suddenly woken out of a deep sleep he could immediately have told you how much such *boccaccino* cost by the yard. It was also clear to him that the girl had dropped the handkerchief for him to pick up and hand to her, and that she would stop and affect an air of great surprise – Yes, that really is my handkerchief, I didn't notice I dropped it, thank you, sir, where did you find it? – and with that the ice would have been broken and they would be well away. Little stratagems of that kind were resorted to by women in south and north alike, and the women of Milan in particular had the reputation of being light-hearted and always ready for love.

A delightful little Annie, he said to himself, for to him every girl he fancied was a little Annie, even though her name turned out to be Giovanna, Maddalena, Beatrice or, in an eastern country, Fatima or Julmar. But now there's no time to lose, he said to himself, noticing that his Annie was no longer walking ahead of him, he could not see her, she had vanished. So dismayed and bewildered was he by this that he let himself be jostled and sworn at by the mule drivers and porters for quite a while with the handkerchief in his hand before he realized that this so promising adventure was over before it had really begun.

Well, it's her fault and not mine if she doesn't get her handkerchief back, he said to himself, disappointed and in a foul temper. Made of the best *boccaccino* and hardly used . . . you don't just abandon a thing like that. Why was she in such a hurry? The devil take me, she might at least have looked round to see if I were there. Jesus, what eyes, what a face. Damn it, I should have been quicker off the mark.

As he castigated the girl and himself like this, blaming first himself then her for his having lost sight of her, it struck him that, as she had vanished anyway, he might as well have a closer look at that strange admirer of hers in the market place – it might perhaps be a good idea to strike up an acquaintanceship with him. That way it might perhaps be possible to find out something about her and what she was like, he said to himself, where she lived, her habits and her family, where he might be able to meet her again, and whether she was a respectable girl or one of the easy sort. For it was always a good idea to know what sort of water one was fishing in.

Meanwhile the singer in the market place had got down from his barrel, and when Joachim Behaim approached he was surprised to find that this man, who had been acting like a love-sick youth and had amused the donkey drivers with his song, was quite elderly, long passed fifty in fact. He did not look remotely like a lover, and was just about as gaunt as death itself, and Behaim had the impression that somewhere in the course of his travels he had come across him before. That must have been long ago and in another country. France, perhaps? At Troyes? Or Besançon? Or could it have been in Flanders or Burgundy? No, he could not remember the place or the occasion of their previous encounter, which seemed to have the remoteness of a dream. But the more he thought about it the more certain he felt that this was not the first time he had set eyes on that face, in which years, experience, passions, as well as disappointments and many cares, had left deep furrows.

The man seemed to have noticed that Joachim Behaim was approaching him and wanting to talk to him. He looked over Behaim's head with raised eyebrows and he assumed an expression of cold rebuff. As proud as a man being led to the gallows, Behaim said to himself, at the same time conscious of the absurdity of the idea, because no one walked to the gallows proudly, but piteously, appealing for sympathy, or perhaps even indifferently if he were reconciled to his fate. But this man with his arrogant expression looked as if he would take any questions about the girl very much amiss, as if, indeed, he were disinclined to talk to anyone about anything. Perhaps he would welcome an opportunity for a quarrel, and in fact from the look of him his blade sat very loosely in its sheath.

Behaim was not lacking in courage and was well able to take care of himself in a rough-house, but he was inclined to be cautious, and he preferred to keep out of trouble in a city in which he was a friendless stranger. So he walked past without speaking to the man or giving him another glance.

Since then he had not seen the girl again, and he had not gone every day to the Via San Jacopo, for selling the two horses had kept him busy. But as soon as that difficult deal was completed and he could dismiss it from his mind, he left the inn where he was staying, though it offered him all the comfort and convenience that he wanted and was entitled to expect in a foreign country, and rented a big attic bedroom in the Via San Jacopo from a man who traded in wax candles.

He spent a whole afternoon looking down at the street from his attic window, but the girl did not appear. It struck him that, if she did appear, by the time he had hurried down the spiral staircase and through the room the candle-dealer used to store his wares she would certainly have vanished again, and he kicked himself for not having thought of this before. He also assured himself that he had stayed on in Milan for something far, far more important than the girl, who was merely a minor and incidental concern in comparison with the all-important matter of recovering his money at last. When he was tired of waiting and looking out of the window, and as it was getting dark into the bargain, he went downstairs to consult the candle-dealer.

The latter was a very simple man who never looked beyond

his shop door, but he was talkative and full of his own importance; and when he started talking to someone he did not easily let him go. This "German" was grist to his mill.

"Come in, come in," he began. "Sit down and make yourself comfortable, and tell me where the shoe pinches. For I have lived long enough in this city to be able to give you all sorts of information and advice and thus be of assistance to you. Are you here to sell or to buy, and if so, what? If it's to buy, my first piece of advice to you, sir, is to be very careful. Don't buy anything without consulting me first, for this city has greater lords, greater stones and greater rogues than any other, as the saying is. Or have you any health troubles, are you suffering from any complaint requiring an apothecary or a physician? You look as if a little bleeding would do you good."

"I'm here to look for a man who for a long time has owed me money for goods bought from my father," said Behaim when it was his turn to speak. "And I've always been rather plethoric, though I feel very well on it."

"So you're looking for a man who owes you money for goods supplied by your father," the candle-dealer repeated as slowly and portentously as if this piece of information required some hard thinking on his part, though first he must commit it to memory word for word. "What sort of goods?" he then asked.

"Small silver boxes for keeping needles in," Behaim explained. "Also slippers of the kind that in Venice are called *zoccoli*."

"*Zoccoli, zoccoli*," the candle-dealer repeated, as if he were allowing the word to sink deeply into his consciousness. "And silver boxes, did you say? Are you sure the man's still alive?"

"The man who owes me the money?" said the German. "Yes, I'm told he's still alive."

"That's a pity," said the candle-dealer. "It's awkward for me, and I'm afraid I may not be able to help you in this case. Really, it's most unfortunate. I supply candles for funeral services, that is my business, and that is why I find out about people here in Milan only when they are dead, for only then does one find out who they were and what their business was during their lifetime."

"Really? Is that so?" Behaim exclaimed in surprise.

"But if he's still alive," the candle-dealer went on, "my advice to you is to apply to a member of the porters' guild and ask him to help you. For here in Milan porters go to every house and see what goes on behind the scenes, and there's nothing they don't know. But see that you don't pick on one who has loaded too many boxes and bales on his back, because he'll be no use – he's not the type to make do with 'Hey, watch out!' or 'Out of my way!': that sort can easily be rude, and if he merely wishes a plague on you or hopes you die of apoplexy or rotting teeth, you can say you got off lightly. There's nothing you won't hear from the porters of Milan."

"There's something else I want to ask you," Behaim said. "Several days ago I was walking down this street wanting to find something nice and agreeable for the evening . . ."

"Something nice and agreeable for the evening?" the candle-dealer exclaimed enthusiastically. "If that's what you want, that's no problem. That's something right up my street. Go and buy a couple of lampreys. They're just the thing for spoilt palates, and they're right in season. I'll cook them for you while you fetch the wine, and we'll have a pleasant evening together. I'll tell a story, then you'll tell a story . . ."

"But what I wanted for the evening was not lampreys, but a girl," Behaim interrupted. "An attractive girl, and I was lucky, I met one whom I really liked. But I lost sight of her and couldn't find her again. But I think she must often have passed your shop door, and if I describe her to you, maybe you'll be able to tell me who she is."

"Be quick about it, then," the candle-dealer encouraged him, "but keep it brief, or the lampreys will all have gone. This time you're applying to the right person, because I know all the girls in this neighbourhood, I still know them from the time when I was thinking of marrying. Believe it or not, they were after me in swarms, just like thrushes when the grapes are ripe."

"How long ago was it when you were thinking of marrying?"

"Years ago," the candle-dealer replied with a sigh. "Let me think. Yes, it must have been about twelve to fifteen years ago. You're perfectly right. Time is the great destroyer, second only to death, and you can't tell from vinegar that once upon a time it was wine."

"The girl I met in this street was young and very pretty," Behaim announced. "Tall, and with a good figure. And that little nose of hers . . ."

He stopped, not really knowing what else to say about the girl.

". . . fitted her face quite exceptionally well," he went on. "And she wasn't the least bit stuck up either: she smiled at me and dropped her handkerchief for me to pick up, this one here made of good *boccaccino*."

"Ugh! What a hussy! Gives men the come-hither? She'll do you no credit."

"Now watch your language," the German said, flaring up. "What right have you to talk about her? Anyway, who's talking about credit? I want her, that's all. What has anyone's credit got to do with it? If the soup's good, what do I care about the plate?"

"All right, all right," the candle-dealer, who didn't want to be cheated of his lampreys, said to pacify him. "It's your business and not mine. Do what you like with her."

"But I haven't got as far as that yet," Behaim complained. "I only saw her once and haven't found her since."

"You'll see her, you'll see her as often as you like," the candle-dealer assured him. "All you need do is pass her house, she'll be craning her neck at the window or, if she knows you're coming, she'll be sitting on the wall in front of the house like the Holy Virgin all dressed up for the Assumption."

"But the trouble is," said Behaim, "that I don't know where she lives or where to look for her."

"Where to look for her?" the candle-dealer exclaimed. "Here, there and everywhere, of course, in this street and that street, in the churches, the markets, in front of the stalls, everywhere. There are plenty of places to look for her, Milan's a big city."

"It occurs to me that perhaps there is a way that might lead to her," said Behaim.

"There are a hundred ways," said the candle-dealer, as if their abundance was to Behaim's advantage.

"She seems to know a man whom I can describe to you exactly, for I observed him closely," Behaim went on. "He's a tall, lean fellow, hollow-cheeked and hook-nosed, no longer young, and he wears stockings of grey buck's leather and a worn old coat with some velvet trimming; and sometimes he stands up and sings over there in the market."

"Stands up in the market and sings?" exclaimed the candle-dealer. "And when he's drunk, dances the galliard, doesn't he? I know the man you want. Certainly I do. He's a kind of poet, he recites his own verse, and he places his words as deftly as a weaver throws his shuttle. He's not one of our people, he's said to come from around Aosta, or even farther away, but he dances the galliard as only someone born in Lombardy can. I don't know what he's called, or what name he answers to, but he's to be found every evening at the Lamb, where he sits with the painters, musicians, writers of lampoons and the stone-masons from the Cathedral, kicking up a din that can be heard all over the neighbourhood."

"I'm very much obliged to you," Behaim said. "I'm looking for amusing company this evening."

"And you shall have it," said the candle-dealer, "the best you could possibly find. Now go and buy the lampreys while I make up the fire. You get the wine, I still have some mutton in the house. You don't know me, but when I'm in the mood you won't stop laughing the whole evening at the jokes I'll tell you. Wouldn't you like to hear how I once diddled a whore out of her fee?"

The German rubbed his left arm with his right hand, as he always did when something did not really appeal to him.

"Another time," he then announced. "Today you must

excuse me. I really am very much obliged to you. But where am I to find the Lamb?"

"That's not something you should ask me," said the disappointed candle-dealer. "I'm not one who spends his money in taverns. If you prefer those people's company to mine, so be it. Go to the Cathedral square, wander round a bit, and when you hear an infernal din from somewhere or other, go towards it. You're a stranger in the town, and you know I'm at your service with any information you require. But if you want information about taverns, you must ask others, not me."

Chapter 3

Joachim Behaim escaped from the relentless rain through the low door of the Lamb inn. His eyes immediately sought out the fire in the hearth, and when he saw the brushwood piled up round it he closed the door behind him with pleasure and relief, for on a cold, wet evening like this nothing pleased him better than a blazing wood fire. The landlord was evidently not stingy with firewood, though he was with oil – for only one of the two lamps suspended by iron chains from the ceiling was alight, and it dimly illuminated the big room with its corners and recesses. Nevertheless when Behaim glanced round he saw at once that the man he was looking for was not there. About ten customers were sitting at round wooden tables, drinking and talking noisily. Among them were some who were very respectably dressed in the Spanish or French fashion, while others were as poorly and shabbily dressed as if they had had no wages for a long time. Some had come wearing leather aprons and clogs, and one man, who was sitting apart and drawing geometrical figures with chalk on the table, was in a friar's habit. Behaim paid his respects to them all by bowing right and left, cap in hand, as he entered.

The landlord, a big, heavy man, emerged from his corner, relieved Behaim of his soaking coat, and asked what he could do for him. At the same time one of the customers rose and went behind Behaim where, unseen by him, he crossed himself three times, as people sometimes do when they see a notorious thief and gallows-bird in the street. Some of the customers – stone-masons, painters, woodcarvers and musicians – had agreed to play a trick on the landlord that would result in his being beaten up or at least receiving a few kicks. They happened to have been talking about a man who had been systematically working his way through the inns and eating houses of the city, ordering the most expensive dishes—capons, meat pies, pastries – and the dearest wines, and then disappearing without paying. At the landlord's request they had agreed to warn him in this way if the man appeared at his inn, and that is what they had done when Behaim appeared on the scene.

"You can bring me some wine, and I want the best," Behaim said to the landlord, who was looking him straight in the eye.

"Yes, the best, as I expected," the landlord exclaimed, angered by what he took to be the newcomer's impudence. "And perhaps smoked lamb or a capon with a ragout of fine mushrooms? There's just one thing I want to say, sir. I know what I know, and I have eyes everywhere. No one takes a step without my knowing it. I know how to keep my eyes open, and if I had been on guard at Christ's tomb, He would not have risen."

Behaim looked at him in surprise and said nothing; he could not understand what all this was about, or why his wine was not brought immediately. But one of the master-masons sitting there in leather apron and clogs called out in a friendly, relaxed fashion, like someone who has the advantage of superior knowledge: "He would have risen."

"He would not, He would have had second thoughts about it," the landlord replied indignantly, for he resented doubt being cast on his vigilance.

"He would have risen, I tell you," the master-mason insisted, seeming to imply that in spite of his vigilance the German was going to get away without paying.

"Perhaps He might have, but not before I'd broken every bone in His body," exclaimed the landlord, infuriated by the master-mason's persistence in contradicting him; and when he said this he was no longer thinking about Christ, but only about the German who, he supposed, was determined to cheat him.

Meanwhile the man in friar's habit had raised his head from his geometrical figures.

"Why is he shouting like that? What's it all about?" he wanted to know.

"The glorious resurrection of Christ, reverend Brother Luca," the master-mason replied amicably but respectfully too, for Brother Luca taught mathematics at Pavia University.

"And is it the risen Christ you are making such a din about?" asked the learned friar, turning to the landlord.

"Yes, and that's my business and not yours," the landlord replied. "This is my house, and I'm responsible for what goes on here. I don't concern myself with your drawings and figures, after all, except to sponge the table clean and leave it fit for a Christian customer after you've gone."

But the friar had gone back to his mathematics and was no longer listening.

"Landlord, I'm still waiting for my wine," Behaim said, "and what that has to do with the Resurrection I don't know. Perhaps there is a connection that I can't see, but I didn't come here to discuss theology. Take my coat to the kitchen and hang it up to dry in front of the fire. We'll talk about the smoked lamb later, but I don't eat mushrooms."

The landlord now looked at the coat and noticed to his surprise that it was of the best quality cloth, besides being trimmed with expensive fur; it was certainly worth more than anything he could serve the German with in one evening, and it dawned on him that the other customers had been pulling his leg.

"You shall have your wine right away, sir, and the best that I have, my Vino Santo from Castiglione, for the sake of which people come to me from far and wide, even from Pavia, like the reverend gentleman there, who tried to butt in just now – so much the worse for him. No one gets the better of me," he went on, raising his voice so as to be heard by everyone. "I wasn't born yesterday, I can size a fellow up at a glance. I shan't be a moment, sir, I'm on my way."

He made his way down to the cellar to fill a stone jug with Vino Santo, head held high and without deigning to glance at his enemies.

After tasting the wine Joachim Behaim felt very cosy indeed. I could do with some of this every evening, he said to himself, and there ought to be a jug full of it by my bedside every night, wherever I am. He leaned back in his chair and shut his eyes, and the painters' and master-masons' talk went on round him. The things they talked about were remote from anything in his experience.

". . . that's why I should prefer to paint her as Leda, in the nude and with downcast eyes . . ."

"With the swan in her lap?"

"Would you believe it? What sort of people would accept a commission like that?"

"I spent no less than eleven lire on indigo, white lead and gold."

"In the nude, but on one side . . ."

". . . and he opened the chest, put his head inside as if he were going to disappear into it, and I thought he was just going to come up with the money . . ."

". . . covered with three veils, that's a very difficult thing to paint, it will give me a chance to show what I can do . . ."

"And with the swan in her lap?"

"An armourer. A master potter. Would you believe it? And a bombard-maker."

"And he produced a piece of cloth from the chest. He wanted to give me a piece of cloth for a suit instead of the money. That's what he offered me, who have enhanced the reputation of this city with my art."

"It'll take two years to do the three."

"He's an idiot. He's a skinflint. I felt like bashing him over the head with his cloth."

"If you're not well in with the powers-that-be in this city, who have such fine commissions to hand out . . ."

"He's mean."

"With the swan in her lap?"

"Yes, with the swan in her lap? Is that so important? Anyone can paint in a fowl like that."

"There's Mancino. He's kept us waiting a long time this evening. Mancino, come here."

"He wouldn't have come sooner even if the Pope had sent for him. He's been with that fat girl he's crazy about."

"He walks in like a hero, straight from the battlefield of love . . ."

". . . from the bordel in which they both reside."

"Quite right, quite right. That's exactly where I've come from. Any objection, anyone?"

Behaim's tipsy sleepiness vanished, for he recognized the newcomer's deep, resonant voice. He opened his eyes. The man who had sung in the market place, the man with the lined face and burning eyes, was standing in the room, declaiming:

> Say that you love me, and no sooner said
> Than with rekindled passion I replied:
> "Into a paradise I'll turn your bed
> In the bordel in which we both reside."

"Landlord," he interrupted himself as he sat down at his friends' table. "Give me what you can for a three-copper piece, but be careful about what you set before me, for more than that copper coin I do not have in my pocket, but the coin is genuine and of full weight. But where was I?"

> Triumphant, like Achilles in his day,
> The battle won, and with a victor's pride,
> I left her sleeping when I came away
> In the bordel in which we both reside.

"We've all heard those verses from you more than a dozen times," said one of the customers sitting at the man's table, "and even the landlord knows them by heart. Think up some new verses, Mancino, and perhaps there'll be supper for you as a result."

Behaim beckoned to the landlord.

"Who's the man who's just come in?" he asked. "The one with the three-copper piece. He looks a strange fellow."

"Him?" said the landlord contemptuously. "You're not the first that doesn't like the look of him. He's a versifier, a poet, and he recites his poems to earn himself a meal. They call him Mancino, because he does everything with his left hand, even with a sword he cuts and thrusts with his left, he's a violent man and he's quick on the draw. No one knows his real name, and he doesn't even know it himself, because he was found one morning lying in the road with a cracked skull. They took him to the surgeon, and when he came round he had lost his memory, he couldn't remember anything whatever of his past life, he couldn't even remember his name. Strange, isn't it, sir, that a man could forget his name. Messer Leonardo, who often comes here and talks to him . . . What, sir, you don't know who Messer Leonardo is? Messer Leonardo, who made the bronze statue of the late duke's horse? You've never heard of him? Permit me to ask where you come from, sir, from Turkey? A man like that Leonardo is born once in a century, perhaps. He's a supreme genius, a supreme genius in all the arts and sciences. I'm an innkeeper, sir, where I'm most at home is in my kitchen, and no one knows more about buying wine than I do, don't ask me, ask others, ask anyone you like in Milan about Messer Leonardo the Florentine, ask Brother Luca over there or Master d'Oggiono, the painter, who's sitting with the *mancino*, yes, quite right, the left-handed man we're talking about. Messer Leonardo says it's because of the injury to his skull and his anatomy that he can't remember his name or where he comes from. Sometimes he thinks he remembers, and imagines he's the son of a duke or some other nobleman, and had been travelling for pleasure and owned town houses and country estates, fish ponds and woods, and had jurisdiction over several villages, and it's all waiting for him, though he doesn't know where. At other times he complains that he has never been anything but a penniless vagabond, that he has suffered greatly from hunger, cold and other troubles, and has had several narrow escapes from the gallows. God alone knows the truth. He has been coming here for years, his friends sometimes pay for his supper and sometimes don't. Well, a slice of bread and some sausage doesn't worry me. The Italian he talks is like that of people from the mountains of Savoy; perhaps that's where his duchy is, or perhaps it's on the moon. He's said to spend the day with dissolute women, and I don't know anything else about him, that's all I know."

He took away Behaim's jug to refill it. The man he had been talking about was leaning back in his chair, gazing at the smoke-blackened ceiling from which the landlord's sausages hung. Now he turned to the man sitting next to him.

"You're quite right to complain that I bore you with verse you already know,' he said. "So I've composed something new that perhaps won't entirely displease you. Here is the ballad of the things that I know and the one thing I don't know."

"Listen to Mancino's ballad about the things that . . . Well, begin then, all's quiet, everyone's listening."

The landlord, who was coming back with the refilled wine jug, stopped in the doorway and listened.

"But there's a gentleman here," Mancino went on, bowing in the direction of Behaim's table, "who is known to nobody here and may perhaps not be willing to listen to my verse. He may perhaps wish to drink his wine in peace."

Behaim, realizing that this was meant for him as everyone looked at him, rose quickly to his feet and said that he wanted to hear the verse as much as everyone else, and he added that drinking his wine alone gave him little pleasure and that he had come here in the hope of being able to join in interesting conversation, and his name was Joachim Behaim.

"So don't stand on ceremony and come and join us, and we'll drink and be merry." The invitation came from a man with a bald head and a greying moustache who was sitting with Mancino. "My name is Giambattista Simoni, I'm a woodcarver, and you can see a young Christ of mine in the Cathedral in the first side chapel on the right coming from the main entrance. Here in the Lamb I'm the novice master."

The devil take me if now I don't find out where to find that Annie of mine, Behaim muttered to himself, going over to the table, holding his cap with one hand and his chair with the other. He repeated that his name was Joachim Behaim. He listened to the names of the others and promptly forgot them, and sat down next to the bald woodcarver who had described himself as the novice master.

"To closer acquaintance," the latter said, and drank his health. "Have you been to the Cathedral?" he added in the same breath, for he, like all Milanese, was proud of that great symbol they had erected in God's honour and their own.

"No, I attended Mass in the Dominican church; it was convenient for me, only a few paces away, but not any more, because where I now live my church is San Jacopo, though that's not quite so near, because I moved from my inn to the Via San Jacopo only today."

After giving this information to satisfy the novice master's curiosity, he leant across the table and tried to strike up a conversation with Mancino.

"If my memory doesn't deceive me, sir," he said, "I saw you in the market a few days ago . . ."

"What can I do for you, sir?" replied Mancino, who had been mentally polishing his verses.

"In the vegetable market. You were standing on a barrel . . ." Behaim went on.

"The ballad of the things I know," Mancino announced, rising to his feet. "There are three verses, followed as usual by a short envoi."

". . . and singing," Behaim persisted. "And the girl that went by . . ."

"Quiet! Quiet for Mancino," the master-mason at the next table called out so loudly that he startled Brother Luca, who was still absorbed in his geometrical figures, while the landlord, who had just filled Behaim's pewter goblet, froze like a statue with the jug in his hand.

Mancino had climbed on to a chair. The dim lamplight fell

on his lined face. All was quiet, except for ghosts wailing in the canopy over the hearth. He began:

> I know the priest by his apparel,
> I know the master by the man;
> The wine by glancing at the barrel
> The vanity of life's brief span.
> I know praise and I know blame,
> Stabs in the back, the lightning blow;
> I know honour, vice and shame;
> Only myself I do not know.

The landlord lowered the jug, which had become too heavy for him. The two master-masons sat like weary Titans, staring down at their clogs, the one propping his chin on his fist, the other, his brow. Brother Luca had raised his scholarly head, and without realizing it used his chalk to beat time with the rhythm of the verse. And Mancino went on:

> I know heaven, I know hell;
> Flies in soup and mouldy bread,
> Money in my purse as well,
> Ditch or haystack for a bed.
> Drinks for which I never paid,
> Bailiffs to catch me far too slow;
> Beauty that had still to fade;
> Only myself I do not know.
>
> I know the sword-blade's cut and thrust,
> I know the whores that walk the streets;
> I know what love is and what lust,
> The coward's fears, the hero's feats.
> I know crimes without redress,
> I know the gipsy's wiles and know
> Drunken sprees, forgetfulness;
> Only myself I do not know.

> I know the harsh vicissitudes of life:
> I know too well brute death's relentless flow.
> I know life's joys, its sorrows and its strife;
> I know it all, myself I do not know.

"That envoi sums it all up," said Mancino, jumping down from the chair. "It puts in a nutshell all that I have to say on the subject, and the three preceding verses are as superfluous as most of what flows from poets' mouths and pens. But I have an excellent excuse, I was singing for my supper."

The landlord awoke from his trance and put the stone jug of Vino Santo in front of Mancino. "I'm not very well up in the fine arts, as you know," he said, "but I can tell from Brother Luca's expression – he is a professor – that you have composed something very good there. Of course you shouldn't have told a landlord that you know the wine by glancing at the barrel. That was a tall story. May you be forgiven. Just try this for once."

And he went back to the cellar to fetch wine for Behaim.

Mancino's companions found little to say about his poem, but what they thought about it was evident from their nods and gestures, the glances they exchanged, and the way they drank his health. One after another they extracted small silver coins or a few coppers from their pockets, laid them together, and called for fish and meat for Mancino.

The landlord came back. Something had struck him on the way to the cellar. He went over to Behaim to serve him, and whispered in his ear:

"Did I exaggerate, sir? He's a genius, one of the greatest, as I told you. Only you mustn't believe that about mouldy bread and flies in the soup. Flies in the soup? In my inn? That you mustn't believe. True, bread can go mouldy if it's damp, but then I don't offer it to my guests. But that's what poets are like. If they need a rhyme, they don't worry about destroying an honest man's reputation. Flies in the soup? In my house? Drinks he didn't pay for – there he spoke the truth for once. About that, not about flies in the soup . . ."

"Now leave me in peace for a moment," Behaim interrupted.

"All right, the wine is on the house," the landlord, unable to stop talking straight away, said more to himself than to Behaim. "I said so, and I keep my word, in spite of all that about flies . . . Yes, gentlemen, I'm just coming, here I am, he shall be served immediately."

The woodcarver turned to Behaim again.

"You come from over the mountains?" he asked, pointing over his shoulder with his thumb as if Germany lay somewhere behind his back. "Over the Albula and the Bernina?"

"That would have been an arduous journey at this time of year," said Behaim, emptying his pewter mug at a single draught. "No, sir, I came across the sea from the east, from the territories of the Grand Turk. I've been on a business trip to Aleppo, Damascus, the Holy Land and Alexandria."

"What? In Turkish territory? And they didn't impale you? They didn't flay you?" the woodcarver exclaimed in surprise.

"They don't do so much flaying and impaling when they're at home," said Behaim, pleased at being regarded as a prodigy by everyone.

The woodcarver thoughtfully stroked his moustache.

"But they're said to be continually wallowing in Christian blood," he said.

"When they do business they are very polite," Behaim explained. "They're not so different from you Milanese when someone comes to buy your armour or your haberdashery. Would you impale or flay him? Or would the Sienese do that to customers interested in buying their marzipan or confectionery? Besides, I have a letter signed by the Sultan which ensures that I am treated well and with proper respect."

Mancino looked at Behaim with sudden interest.

"Do you think the Turks will be invading Italy next year?" he asked.

Behaim shrugged his shoulders and picked up his mug.

"They're building a huge fleet against Venice and have taken experienced sea captains into their service," he announced.

"Heaven preserve us," one of the stone-masons exclaimed.

"If they swallow Venice for breakfast, they'll gobble up Milan for supper."

"As the threat is so imminent, the time has come at last to send someone with a ready tongue and experience in the interpretation of Holy Scripture to the temporary residence of the Grand Turk . . ."

"There he goes again," the painter d'Oggiono, still a very young man with brown hair falling over his shoulders, exclaimed with a laugh. "He's had that idea in his head for years," he explained to Behaim. "He thinks he's the man for the job, and wants to convert the Grand Turk to the love of Christ and the worship of His divinity."

"It would be a magnificent task to tackle," Mancino said with flashing eyes.

"I should drop that idea if I were you," said Behaim. "The Turks are very peculiar about their faith." He tapped the table with his empty mug to summon the landlord.

"Personally," d'Oggiono said, "I should have more confidence in the under-water diving device suggested by Messer Leonardo to hole the enemy ships when they approach our shores."

"But so far," the organist and composer Martegli pointed out, "he has obstinately refused to hand over to the military his plans for his device, in view of men's evil nature, he says, which could lead to the sinking of ships together with their crews."

"That's true," said Brother Luca, without raising his eyes from his drawings, "and let me repeat his words, for they are worth remembering. 'If,' he wrote, 'the structure and equipment of the human body seem so marvellous to you, consider, O man, that the body is nothing in comparison with the soul that inhabits that structure. For the latter, whatever it may be, is God's thing. Let it therefore dwell in His works in accordance with His will and pleasure, and do not allow your anger and your wickedness to destroy a life. For truly he who does not value life does not deserve to possess it.' "

"Who is this Messer Leonardo?" Behaim wanted to know.

"This is the second time I've heard him mentioned this evening. Is he the one who made the late duke's bronze horse? At all events, he strings words together very skilfully."

"That's the man," d'Oggiono replied. "I was his pupil, and whatever I can do I owe to him. You'll never come across anyone like him, nor will anyone else, for to make another like him is beyond Nature's power."

"He's impressive to look at," said the woodcarver. "You may perhaps see him here this evening, because he knows that when Brother Luca's in Milan he spends his evenings at the Lamb."

"You can't be quite so sure of that about me," said Brother Luca. "At any rate there's no mathematical certainty about it, because sometimes I go to the Bell. But there the tables are so smooth that you can't draw on them with chalk."

Meanwhile Behaim remembered that he was not there because of Messer Leonardo, and so, in pursuit of his real objective, he tackled Mancino again.

"Now, about that girl . . ." he began by way of introducing the subject.

"What girl?" Mancino replied over his empty plates.

"The one that walked past the market and smiled at you."

"Keep quiet, don't breathe a word about her," Mancino whispered with an uneasy glance at d'Oggiono and the woodcarver, who were earnestly discussing the Lamb, the Bell and mathematics with Brother Luca.

"You could tell me her name," said Behaim in similarly muffled tones. "It's the kind of favour one man can do another."

"Please don't talk about her," Mancino said very quietly, but in a distinctly unpromising manner.

"You could at least tell me where I could find her again," said Behaim, who was nothing if not persistent.

"That I don't know," said Mancino, slightly raising his voice, but so that only Behaim could hear. "What I can tell you is the state you'll be in when you do find her: you'll be creeping on all fours after what I do to you."

At this Behaim flared up.

"Sir," he said, "you are permitting yourself the impermissible."

"Hey, what's this? A row?" exclaimed d'Oggiono, whose attention had been attracted by these last words, which had been spoken aloud.

"A row? Well, it all depends," said Mancino, looking fixedly at Behaim with his hand on the hilt of his dagger. "I said it would be a good idea to open the window to let in a little fresh air, and this gentleman said it should stay shut. Let it stay shut, for heaven's sake."

"Go ahead and open it, for heaven's sake," Behaim said grumpily, drinking up his wine, and Mancino's hand dropped from the hilt of the dagger.

For a short while there was silence, and to break it d'Oggiono asked: "Are you in Milan on business?"

"Not exactly," Behaim replied. "I'm here to collect some money from someone who has owed it me for years."

"For a small fee, sir, I'll collect it for you," said Mancino, as if nothing had happened between them. "Leave it to me, sir, and you won't have to lift a finger. As you know, I'm always at your service."

Behaim, who thought his leg was being pulled, looked at him morosely, but took no more notice of him. The wine was beginning to go to his head – he had already drunk too much – but he was still master of his words and actions, and whether for better or worse he wanted to have nothing further to do with this individual who was so ready with his dagger. So he began talking to d'Oggiono about what was on his mind.

"The man who owes me the money is a Florentine now living in Milan. His name is Bernardo Boccetta. Perhaps you can tell me how to find him."

For all reply d'Oggiono threw back his head and burst out laughing, as did the others. They seemed to be extremely amused by what this German had said. Only Mancino did not laugh. He kept his eyes fixed on Behaim, and his face expressed astonishment and concern.

"I don't see what's funny about it," Behaim remarked crossly. "He owes me seventeen ducats. Seventeen ducats, genuine and of full weight."

"Sir, one can tell you're a stranger in Milan," d'Oggiono said. "You don't know Boccetta, or you'd devote your time to more pressing business."

"What do you mean?" Behaim asked.

"That your money is lost – you might as well have thrown it into the sea."

To Behaim these words were like a stab to the heart.

"Rubbish," he said. "I've got written proof of the debt."

"Then take good care of it," said d'Oggiono.

"And so I shall," said Behaim with a leaden tongue, for the wine was rumbling more and more loudly in his head. "It's worth seventeen ducats."

"It's not worth seventeen hoots," d'Oggiono said with a laugh.

The woodcarver put his hand on Behaim's shoulder. "If you live as long as a crow," he said, "you won't get a single hoot from Boccetta."

"Leave your hoots out of this. I'll see that I get my money."

"Let me tell you about Boccetta," the woodcarver went on. "So far he has cheated everyone with whom he has dealt. He has gone bankrupt twice, and both times the bankruptcy was fraudulent. He has been in prison and got out without accepting any liability. Everyone knows he's a rogue and a swindler, but nobody can catch him. When you ask for your money back he'll give you words and nothing but words, and when you leave him he'll laugh at you behind your back, and that's all you'll get from him."

Behaim banged his fist on the table. "I'm the man to deal with a hundred people like that," he said. "You'll see that I get my rights. I'll bet on it two ducats to one."

"Two ducats to one?" d'Oggiono exclaimed. "I'll take that. Is it a deal?"

"Yes," said Behaim, shaking d'Oggiono's hand across the table.

"You could take him to court," the organist Martegli pointed out. "That you could do, to be sure, and the lawyers would take your money, and that's all that would come of it. Think about what I've said. Shame and disgrace have no effect on him."

"Who are you?" Behaim asked in a drunken haze. "I don't know you. Why are you meddling in my affairs?"

"I beg your pardon," said the organist, a quiet and retiring individual.

"Boccetta's a queer fish," the woodcarver said. "He lives like the poorest of the poor, he carries his own basket to market when he goes there to buy stale bread and root vegetables, because that's all that ever appears on his table, though he has any amount of money and could live like a prince of the Church. He buries or hides his money, under a pile of rusty nails or somewhere. He lives like a pauper, out of fear that one day he might become one."

"He's like a leech," said Behaim.

"Yes, he's a real leech," the woodcarver agreed.

"I'm a leech myself when I attach myself to someone," Behaim said, pointing to his breast. "He won't have an hour's peace. Not an hour's peace. And I shan't . . ."

His thoughts grew confused. He tried to rise to his feet, but failed. He told himself that it was time to go home, even if it was on all fours, for he could not manage to walk upright like other people. For a short while he remained gazing into space, and then recalled what he had wanted to say: "I shan't leave Milan until I get my money."

"In that case," said one of the two master-masons, moving closer to him, "you'd do well to order your gravestone from me, for it's here and nowhere else that you'll be buried. Don't take offence, sir, that's my trade."

Joachim Behaim heard these words, but could make no sense of them. The landlord had come over to him and wanted his money. He had to ask three times, and more loudly each time, before Behaim understood. He produced his purse and unsteadily scattered big and small silver coins all over the table-top. The landlord took what he was owed, put the rest back in Behaim's purse, and put the purse in his hand.

Behaim sat there for a time in a drunken stupor, clutching his purse, his eyes closed and his head resting on his chest. Suddenly he heard himself being talked about.

"He's a German, he has just come from the Levant. He's dead drunk. No one knows him, and we don't know what to do with him."

Joachim Behaim yawned, raised his head, and opened his eyes. He saw the man he had seen that morning in the courtyard of the old castle. The man with the Roman nose, the wavy hair, the bushy eyebrows and the huge forehead and intimidating appearance was talking to Brother Luca. Behaim wanted to stand up and bow to him, but could not. His head sank back on to his chest and he fell asleep again.

For a second time fate had put Behaim in Messer Leonardo's path, and on both occasions Behaim was clutching his purse. But Messer Leonardo's thoughts were on his monument to the late duke, whom he had portrayed sitting on a horse.

"He's the dealer from whom Il Moro bought those two fine horses today," he said. "I wish he had come to Milan before. If I had had the big Neapolitan as model for the duke's horse, I'd have made a better job of it."

Chapter 4

The first thing Joachim Behaim noticed when he woke next morning was the surprising fact that he had been using a big, fat tome as a pillow all night. Next he realized he was fully dressed and was lying on a straw sack under a coat he recognized as his own; and, as he lay there wondering how he had got home and why he was lying, not in his own bed, but on a straw sack, he suddenly had an alarming thought, which promptly disappeared when he felt his coat pockets and found that his purse was till in one of them. He rubbed his eyes to drive away his drunken torpor, and noticed for the first time that he was not alone in the room. A man was squatting on the floor with crossed legs like a Turk, busy with a chest that seemed to be standing on two chairs placed side by side, and he was whistling. Behaim was sure the chest had not been in his room the day before, and he could not understand what use he was expected to make of it.

"Out with you," he said calmly but firmly to his landlord, the candle-dealer, who apparently had entered his room unbidden and proposed to go on using it. Behaim wanted to establish once and for all precisely where he drew the line. "What are you doing here, so early in the morning what's more? Take your chest and clear out."

"Good morning," said the man squatting on the floor. "So you're awake, and if you think the laws of hospitality require me to go away and leave you alone, I shall do so with pleasure. But please bear with me for a few minutes, because I don't want to interrupt the job I'm doing just at this moment."

"What sort of behaviour is this?" Behaim exclaimed. "Next

time knock at the door and ask for permission before you come in. That's the sort of behaviour I'm used to."

The man squatting in front of the chest turned his head and pushed the brown hair back from his forehead. He turned out to be holding a paint brush, from which blue paint was dripping on to the floor.

"Why should I ask for permission, sir? Whom do you take me for? At whose door would I be knocking?" he asked.

"By the blood of the holy martyrs, you're right," exclaimed Behaim, quite taken aback. "You're not the person I took you for. But who are you, for heaven's sake, and what are you doing here? I seem to have seen your face somewhere before."

"I'm Marco d'Oggiono, at your service, sir. I'm a painter and former pupil of Messer Leonardo, and last night I was your drinking companion at the Lamb. Don't you remember me now?"

"Of course, of course," Behaim replied, trying vainly to suppress a yawn. "Do forgive me, sir. The fact is, I took you for my landlord, a man of very limited intelligence, but very intrusive and talkative – one of those people you have to keep at arm's length. What he'd say to your dripping blue paint on the floor I've no idea. So you're Signor d'Oggiono. And what happy chance brought you here so early in the morning?"

"Sir," d'Oggiono now said with a trace of impatience, "you still seem to be not quite awake. Put your head in cold water and you'll feel better, the wash basin's over there. You're in my room in my house, and it's my floor I'm dripping paint on."

"So that's why I didn't know where I was when I woke up," exclaimed Joachim Behaim, shaking his head and still rather befuddled.

"Last night there was no way of finding out from you in which inn you were staying, so I brought you back with me," d'Oggiono explained, "and you slept on the straw sack which Brother Luca uses when he spends the night here if the hour's late or the weather bad. What he did last night, I've no idea. But he turned up this morning to borrow two carlini from me, for the good brother is ill-provided with worldly goods. He didn't get them, but he accepted one of my charcoal pencils instead, and he was very satisfied with it. You see, as he's a mathematician, he's also a philosopher, and so is better able to put up with disappointments than people like us are."

Behaim meanwhile took the painter's advice and poured cold water over his head. While washing his hands and face he said:

"Well, Signor d'Oggiono, you performed at least one of the holy works of mercy upon me last night, though it was at the reverend brother's expense, so I'm under an equal obligation to you both. You have also lit a fire in the stove, and that is a second holy work."

"As for the third, which is breakfast," d'Oggiono replied, "the prospects are distinctly poor, unfortunately. All I can offer you is bread and spring onions, followed by half a water melon."

"Bread and spring onions?" Behaim exclaimed. "Do you suppose I normally have trout and truffles for breakfast? Produce the bread and spring onions, and I'll wolf them like a mule driver."

While Behaim ate his breakfast d'Oggiono went back to work on the wooden chest, which was part of the dowry of a wealthy burgher's daughter; his commission was to decorate it with scenes from the Bible, and a Christ, a Madonna and a number of other figures were already discernible on the front of the chest.

"It's always the same," d'Oggiono complained. "They all want the miracle at the wedding-feast of Cana on their chests. I've already done that wretched wedding-feast no fewer than eight times, and I've got a commission for a ninth, and I'm thoroughly sick of that steward of the feast and his stone water-pot. This time I suggested to the girl's father and the bridegroom that, in view of the nature of present-day marriage, I should for a change decorate the chest with Christ's meeting with the woman taken in adultery. But they wouldn't hear of it and insisted on their Miracle of Cana. So let them have it, for heaven's sake. What do you think of that Christ, sir?"

"That Christ? All I can say is that I've never seen a better painting of our Lord," said Joachim Behaim, who had not had much practice in articulating his opinions of paintings or other works of art.

His praise seemed to please d'Oggiono.

"Actually I don't think Messer Leonardo, whose pupil I was, as you know, would be entirely dissatisfied with it," he said. "But, if I told you what I'm being paid for it, you'd be so surprised that you'd make the sign of the cross, there's so little in it for me, particularly when you take into account what an ounce of varnish costs nowadays. These burghers know what's good for them, they bargain and haggle with me as if it were over a waggon-load of timber."

He sighed, glanced at his darned socks and worn shoes, and then set about painting a gold and ochre halo round the head of his Christ.

"I don't bargain and I don't haggle," said Behaim, who by now had finished his breakfast. "I carefully work out the prices of my wares, and in no circumstances will I reduce them by a penny. You have your wares just as I have mine: Christ and the apostles and the Blessed Virgin, the Pharisees, Pilate, the publicans, the sick of the palsy, the lepers and all the womenfolk in the Bible, as well as the holy martyrs and the Three Kings from the East. And I have my wares: Venetian satin and carpets from Alexandria, raisins in pots and saffron and ginger in greased bags. And you ought to do with your wares what I do with mine. The price is such-and-such, and there's no argument about it, and those who don't like it can go their own way. That's what you ought to do with your saints and martyrs, keep to a fixed price. I charge so-and-so much for a well painted Christ, you ought to say, and so-and-so much for a publican or an apostle. If you don't stick to your fixed prices, you'll never be well off, in spite of all your art and all your hard work and all the trouble you take."

"You may well be right," said the painter, who was busy with the Saviour's halo. "I've never thought about it from a business man's point of view. You must also consider, of course, that if they couldn't bargain and haggle with me there are always other artists they could turn to. There are as many artists here as there are peppercorns in Venice, and I should be out in the cold, or out of the frying pan into the fire, as the saying is."

"All right," said Behaim, feeling slightly put out. "Do as you think best, you should know what is good for you. I see it's difficult to advise you."

"The Milanese," d'Oggiono said thoughtfully, "are all suspicious by nature, no one trusts his neighbour, everyone thinks everyone else is out to cheat him and get the better of him, and so they haggle with me just as they haggle with the peasants who take corn, honey, peas or flax to market and really are cheats, for in spite of their simple ways they swindle everyone. You Germans are said to be honest people, and so you are. If you give your word, you keep to it."

He put down his paint brush and looked searchingly at his work, while Behaim rubbed his chin.

"And that's why I'm not worried about those two ducats, though you gave me nothing in writing," d'Oggiono went on after a short pause.

Behaim looked hard at him and stopped rubbing his chin.

"What ducats?" he said.

"I'm referring to our bet at the Lamb last night. You offered me two ducats to one of mine. And don't imagine I'm completely penniless and unable to wager anything. I have some small savings set aside."

"Yes, now I come to think of it I dimly remember shaking hands over a wager of some sort," Behaim muttered, drawing his hand across his brow. "But the devil take me if I can remember what it was about. Wait a minute, let me think. Wasn't it about the Turks, whether they'll be coming to Venice next year?"

"It was about Boccetta. You said he owed you money," d'Oggiono reminded him. "That was what it was about. You claimed you were capable of taking on him and a hundred like him, and that you'd get your money back. And I said . . ."

"Hoots!" Joachim Behaim exclaimed delightedly, giving himself a resounding slap on the thigh. "Didn't you say my claim on him was worth seventeen hoots? I'll show you what sort of hoots they are. Of course, that was what it was about.

You're an honourable man to have reminded me. By my soul, I had completely forgotten all about it."

"So I noticed," said the painter with an embarrassed smile. "And when I said I wasn't worried about your two ducats . . ."

"You'd do better to worry about your one ducat, because you've as good as lost it already," Behaim interrupted. "I've only got to find out where that Boccetta lives, or where to find him, and I'll go and see him straight away. And have your ducat ready for a long journey. Wish it luck and kiss it goodbye, because it will be coming with me to the Levant."

"That, sir, I very much doubt, and have very good reason to do so, though unfortunately I have to admit that my ducats have always been real birds of passage, they've never stayed with me for long. And as for Boccetta, you'll have no difficulty in finding him. All you have to do is to go to the Vercelli gate and keep straight on till you come to some heaps of stones on the left that were once a garden wall. Go through the garden, where you might easily fall into a well that is completely overgrown with thistles. If you manage to avoid that trap, you'll come to a house or, if you prefer it, a mule shed, for it's in a pitiful state – let us just call it four walls and a roof. To put it in a nutshell, all you have to do when you've passed the Vercelli gate is to ask for the house by the well."

"The house by the well beyond the Vercelli gate," Behaim repeated. "That's not hard to remember. And that's where I shall find Boccetta?"

"Yes, that's where you'll find him, assuming he opens the door to you, and assuming you haven't ended up ignominiously at the bottom of the well. And let me tell you straight away how matters will proceed. When you have told him your name and the purpose of your visit, he'll explain that he's far too busy to see you, or he's just going to have his supper, or has an extremely important appointment that it's impossible to postpone, or he's exhausted from the day's work, or he's just about to set out on a pilgrimage to procure indulgences, or he has letters to write or feels ill and must rest – unless he prefers simply to slam the door in your face."

"What do you take me for?" Behaim exclaimed indignantly. "Are you suggesting I don't know how to deal with excuses of that kind? Getting my money is as much a part of my business as mixing paints is of yours. What use would I be if I couldn't manage that?"

He took his coat, inspected it and carefully smoothed it, drew his hand across the expensive fur trimming to remove the bits of straw that had clung to it, and reached for his hat, which d'Oggiono had left overnight on the head of a wood carving of St Sebastian; and finally he went over to the window to see what the weather was like.

The window overlooked a narrow yard with a crop of scrubby grass enclosed between wooden fences. At the far end there was a stable, and in the yard Behaim was surprised to see Mancino with a pail and horse brush curry-combing a piebald horse, while another horse was tethered nearby. Mancino was working hard at the job and did not look up, and once again Behaim had the impression that he had seen that grim, lined face many years before. But he did not linger over this will-o'-the-wisp of a memory, he had the girl on his mind, the girl because of whom he had quarrelled with Mancino the night before. A vision of her walking down the street, smiling and with downcast eyes, rose in his mind, and he lost himself in reverie.

If I go down and talk to Mancino, he said to himself, and give him the handkerchief to hand back to her, she'll know who it was who found it. And if I meet her again she'll stop, or smile at me as she passes, for in Milan girls are allowed all sorts of liberties in relation to men, and I'll say . . . yes, what shall I say to her?

"Woman, what have I to do with thee?"

Behaim turned and stared dumbfounded at d'Oggiono, who had spoken these words, as if something strange and uncanny had happened, as if d'Oggiono had read on his forehead the question in his mind, and he exclaimed huskily: "What's that? What's that? What do you mean? What woman are you talking about?"

"Sir," said d'Oggiono without interrupting his work, "those are the words that Our Lord said to his mother at the wedding at

Cana: 'Woman, what have I to do with thee?' See the Gospel according to St John, right at the beginning, Chapter 2, and in the picture I'm making Him look as if He had just spoken them."

"Quite right, quite right, that's what it says in the Bible," said Behaim, greatly relieved. "And do you also know, sir, that one of your boon companions is down in the yard, the one who threatened me with a dagger last night in the Lamb?"

"Who threatened you with a dagger?" d'Oggiono asked.

"I don't know his real name. The one they call Mancino."

"That's just like him," d'Oggiono explained. "When he's angry he threatens his best friends with the weapon nearest to hand, for he's hot-headed by nature. And he's to be seen every morning about this time down in the yard at work on the two horses that belong to the landlord of the Bell. He knows all about horses, and that's how he earns his midday soup and a few soldi that he spends on women in the brothels. We call him Mancino because he doesn't know his real name himself, and Messer Leonardo says it's a great miracle that anyone could so totally forget his past life because of a brain injury."

"The landlord of the Lamb told me all about that yesterday," Behaim pointed out. "And now it's time for me to go. Thank you for your kindness and hospitality, sir, which I shan't forget, and my best wishes for your work, and think about the advice I gave you, it will be to your advantage. I hope to see you again, in the Lamb, or when I come back to collect my ducat, and until then God bless you, sir, God bless you."

With a flourish of his hat he left and shut the door behind him. Because he had failed to get his two carlini from d'Oggiono, Brother Luca had written in charcoal on the outside of the door the words: "The man who lives here is mean."

"I don't want to hear any complaints about you, so make a good job of it," Behaim said cheerfully to Mancino, thinking that was the best way of starting up a conversation with this poet of the market place, the tavern and the stable while he was grooming a horse.

Mancino looked up, saw who was standing beside him,

grimaced slightly, but answered politely: "Good morning, sir. Were you satisfied with your night's lodging?"

"It was better than I deserved or had any right to expect," Behaim replied. "Had the gentleman up there not taken me in like a true Christian, I should have been picked up out of the gutter this morning."

"That's because you Germans can't distinguish between one wine and another. The one that the landlord of the Lamb offered you yesterday is not one to be drunk by the jugful."

"Quite so," Behaim said. "But it's easy to be wise after the event. And today you're talking to me very sensibly, though yesterday you went for me quite crazily."

"That," said Mancino, "was because you wouldn't stop talking about that girl, though I appealed to you as forcefully as I could to stop it. Because of the friendly feelings and liking I have for the child, I didn't want my friends to get wind of it. They would never have let us hear the end of it, and wouldn't have hesitated to drag the poor girl's reputation through every gutter in the city. So take careful note for the future, sir, not a word about that girl to my friends."

"Really?" Behaim said in surprise. "But your friends seemed to me to be decent, honourable people."

"And so they are, so they are," Mancino replied, quietening the horse, which was getting restive. "They're honourable, decent people, but honourable and decent is something I'm not and never have been. My morals are something it's better not to talk about, and that's the point. The fact of the matter is that my friends think that a girl who doesn't dislike me, one who so much as acknowledges me in the street, must be of the sort that trade their favours for money."

"She doesn't look like that," said Behaim, lost in memory of the girl. "If she were, no price would be too high to pay for her."

"She's as beautiful and pure as a young rose," said Mancino, dipping his horse brush and bare arm in the pail of water.

"She has a good figure and a good complexion, she's not one of your chlorotic types," Behaim admitted. "I won't say that I don't like her. If you could just tell me which church she goes to for Mass . . ."

"So you don't just want me to pimp for you, you want Almighty God to do it too," Mancino said sharply.

"Pimp? Did you say pimp?" Behaim replied angrily. "Speak more respectfully about sacred matters, sir. Surely it's possible to go to Mass without your sharpening your tongue on it. What has pimping got to do with this? I merely want to return her handkerchief. She dropped it and I picked it up."

He produced the *boccaccino* linen handkerchief from his coat pocket and held it under Mancino's nose.

"Yes, that's her handkerchief, I recognize it," Mancino said, carefully taking it between two fingers of his wet hand. "I gave it to her on her saint's day together with a small bottle of perfume. So she dropped it."

"Yes, and you can give it back to her, with a greeting from the man who was walking behind her," Behaim said, "and I don't deny that I should very much like to see her again, I liked her very much, and who knows? It's just possible that she didn't dislike me. But suddenly she had gone with the wind, and what does she expect? That I have time to look for her in all the streets of Milan? My business affairs in Milan prevent it – tell that to my Annie."

"Whom should I tell all this to about your business affairs?"

"To my Annie, of course. Or isn't that her name? You might at least tell me her name."

Mancino ignored the request.

"So you're going to see that Boccetta and ask him for your money?" he said.

"Yes," Behaim said resolutely. "I'm going to see him tomorrow or some other time and settle the matter. And as for the girl, whom it seems, I shall not see again . . ."

"You will see her again," said Mancino, the grief in his face turning to inner fury. "You will see her again, because I can't prevent it. And take note of this: I'm afraid it will turn out badly for the girl. And also for you. And perhaps also for me."

Chapter 5

The house by the well really was in a state of extreme dilapidation, as d'Oggiono had said. It looked as if it had been uninhabited for many years. The roof was decaying, the timbers rotten, the chimney had collapsed, mortar was peeling from the walls, there were cracks everywhere. Behaim knocked and shouted as loudly as he could, but no one opened the door. And as he knocked and waited and shouted and knocked, and again shouted and again waited, he happened to notice a barred window above the door behind which peered a face. The face created the same impression of neglect and decay as the house itself. It was the stubbly and not very clean face of a man who was watching him attentively as he rapped his knuckles sore on the closed door.

"Sir, what is the meaning of this?" Behaim called out angrily. "Why don't you open the door?"

"Why are you making such a row, and on someone else's property, too, and in any case who are you?" the man replied.

"I'm looking for someone of the name of Bocccetta," Behaim explained. "Bernardo Boccetta. I'm told this is the place to find him."

"Everyone wants Bernardo Boccetta," the man said grumpily. "Far too many people want Bernardo Boccetta. Let me see what you've brought before I let you in."

"What I've brought?" Behaim exclaimed in surprise. "What the hell am I supposed to bring you in order to be let in?"

"If you have nothing to pledge, go away," the man at the window called out. "We don't lend anything here on a mere promissory note. Or have you come to redeem a pledge? If so, it's the wrong time, you must come in the afternoon."

"Sir," Behaim replied, "I don't want to borrow money, and I haven't pledged anything with you. All I want is to see Signor Boccetta and nothing else."

"To see Signor Boccetta and nothing else?" exclaimed the man at the window, apparently with great surprise. "Why should you want to see Signor Boccetta if, as you say, you are in no financial difficulties or embarrassment? What is there about him that you want to see? And if you do see him, what then? For I am the Boccetta you want to see."

The German took a step backwards in surprise and had another look at the neglected appearance and sunken features of a man who had once belonged to the Florentine nobility. Then he said with a bow:

"My name is Behaim, sir, and I bring you greetings from my father, Sebastian Behaim, merchant, of Melnik. He will be delighted if I am able to tell him I have been in your house and found you well and prospering."

"You're right, sir, he'll be grateful for any news of me, one hears so seldom from one's friends," Boccetta replied. "Tell him that, so far as my health is concerned, I have nothing to complain about, I'm well, but in other respects – you know yourself what the times are like. What with the talk of war, everything gets more and more expensive, to say nothing of people's envy and resentment and deceitfulness, you have to be patient and take things as they are. It's the will of God, and whether it's going to be worse tomorrow nobody knows. So tell your father, tell him . . ."

"Aren't you going to let me in, sir?" Behaim interrupted.

"Of course. Of course," Boccetta said. "So you're Sebastian Behaim's son. It must be a great joy to have a son to leave behind in the world, but that has not been granted me. Well, when you talk to your father about me, tell him . . ."

"I thought you were going to let me in," said Behaim.

"So I did, and here I am still standing here and talking. Bear with me for just a moment. Where did I put the key? I should like to do honour to my guest as is the custom, but it has just struck me that unfortunately I have nothing in the house to offer you, neither wine nor fruit nor anything else. In these circumstances you might perhaps prefer to avoid putting me to shame and come another time, when I shall be better prepared."

"No, sir," Behaim replied firmly. "I shan't say that I do not appreciate a jug of good wine, but I have been wanting for a long time to have a little chat with you, and I don't want unnecessarily to postpone it, as we don't know what might happen to either of us for, as you so rightly pointed out a few moments ago, we don't know what the morrow may bring. So please don't leave me standing outside your door any longer."

The face disappeared from the window, there was a sound of shuffling footsteps, a chain rattled, a key grated in the lock, and in the open doorway Boccetta tried another excuse.

"As I generally do my business in the morning, I thought . . ."

Behaim cut him short.

"Fine, we can talk business," he said, and walked through the door.

The room into which Boccetta showed his guest could not have been more meagrely furnished. A table, two chairs, a bench with a leg missing, a worm-eaten wooden chest in a corner and two rush mats on the floor, and that was all. A jug of water and a pewter mug stood next to some writing materials on the table. But on the wall there was a Madonna that might have been painted by a good artist, and Behaim went over to look at it.

"Our Lady," Boccetta explained. "I had it from a painter who was at his wits' end because of his debts. For that small picture Master Leonardo, himself a painter, offered me four ducats, cash down. Can you understand how a man who has only to sit down and pick up his brush and a little paint to produce a similar picture or an even better one could offer four ducats for it? Incidentally, Master Leonardo did me the honour of drawing me in his sketch-book."

He then invited Behaim to take a seat, at the same time advising him to be careful.

"Take care not to sit down too heavily," he said. "These chairs are better suited to my weight than to yours. Would you care for a glass of water? It's there ready for you. If my servant were here, I'd send him to the nearest tavern to fetch us both some wine, but I sent him back to his village three weeks ago, for an extra mouth to feed in these times is no trifling matter, believe me."

He sighed, nodded, and started reminiscing: "Yes, sir, those were the days. On Sundays the two of us, your father and I, used to ride out to the villages and farms on our mules, to joke with the peasant girls and give them a pinch on the arm and elsewhere. Your father used to enjoy that, though he looked so respectable that it would have been a pleasure to confess to him. Yes, those were happy days, and business was good, too. But the past is past, and we've reached an age when all passion is spent and we can devote ourselves to the service of God. I've retired from business now, and if I occasionally place my money it's only to use the profit to help the poor. I'm known in the neighbourhood as a friend of God and of all who are in need. But won't you tell me about your business? Perhaps you are thinking of investing money here in Milan? In that case I could help you. I could procure you finance up to any amount at a good rate of interest, or all the securities you might want. And don't talk to me about agent's commission, because anything I did for you would be out of friendship for you and your father. Well, what is the amount you have in mind?"

"The amount I have in mind is seventeen ducats."

"Seventeen ducats? You must be joking. That's ridiculous. You can't be serious? You want to invest seventeen ducats?"

"No, I have come to collect seventeen ducats," Behaim replied. "And from you. There's an entry in our books totalling seventeen ducats due to us that has been there for years, and I've come to collect it from you."

"Seventeen ducats?" said Boccetta. "I know nothing about it."

"You know all about it," Behaim insisted. "I have confirmation here in your own handwriting. Would you like to see it?"

"That's not necessary," Boccetta replied. "If you say so, no doubt there will be justification for what you say. My chief consideration, Signor Behaim, is to keep you and your father happy. But tell me one thing, Signor Behaim; did you subject yourself to the discomforts of a long and arduous journey for such a trivial amount? If someone does such a thing for a good reason or out of piety, I have nothing to say, but . . ."

"I have had other and more substantial business to attend to in Milan," Behaim explained.

Boccetta seemed to be thinking hard for a moment.

"Well, then, that settles it," he said. "Don't worry about the money. You can safely leave it with me. I don't see the slightest risk of your losing it. It's as safe with me as with the Altovici bank, or safer."

"Sir, do you take me for a fool, to fall for that kind of talk?" Behaim exclaimed angrily.

"Why should I take you for a fool?" Boccetta replied. "On the contrary, I was just on the point of putting a sensible proposal to you. Let us say no more about the matter. It's simply not worth causing ill-feeling between two men who esteem and respect each other."

"Be careful, sir," Behaim said with mounting anger. "You have owed me that amount for long enough. If you try to spin it out any longer, so much the worse for you. So much the worse. You don't know me."

Boccetta now looked genuinely concerned.

"Why so violent?" he complained. "Is that the way to talk to someone who has received you hospitably in his house? But for your father's sake I forgive you. That shows how greatly I respect him. And as you seem to attach some importance to the money, sir, you shall have it. In dealing with a friend and a man of honour I can be moulded like wax. At the moment I do not have the money in the house, but come back tomorrow, come back this afternoon. I shall count it out on the table for you, even if I have to sell myself into slavery to raise it."

His regret at not having the money in the house seemed so genuine, his eagerness to settle the matter quickly was so persuasive, that Behaim forgot whom he was dealing with and struck a gentler note. He apologized for having spoken so violently, and added that he was willing to grant Boccetta two days' grace, and with that he took his leave.

When he was outside the house and the door slammed behind him he felt less pleased with himself. He had left empty-handed, had been given nothing but promises, and it struck him that Boccetta had made those promises for the sole purpose of getting him out of the house. He remembered that Boccetta was a pawnbroker. "Let us see what you've brought," he had said. "If you've nothing to pledge, go away." As a pawnbroker he would always have cash in the house.

Joachim Behaim stopped and bit his lip. He was furious at having realized this only when it was too late. And as he walked away, quietly cursing to himself, he heard Boccetta's voice behind him: "Hey, you! Come back, I've something to say to you."

Surprised and pleased, Behaim turned back – but no, the door was not open. Boccetta's face was behind the barred window. He had no intention of letting him in again.

"Your father must have given you travelling expenses. What has happened to them? Have you squandered the lot?" he called out.

Behaim was so taken aback that for a moment he was at a loss for an answer.

"There you stand like a great oaf," Boccetta went on. "What has happened to those expenses? Did you squander the money at cards or spend it all on drink and whores? And now you want to go on enjoying yourself at other people's expense, begging from your father's friends. Aren't you ashamed of yourself? Go away, go away, and may God help you to amend your ways. You're young and strong, you could look for work instead of begging and becoming a burden on people. Seventeen ducats? Is that all? You can have seventeen strokes with a cane."

"Sir," said Behaim, "your impudence leaves me cold. But as you obstinately refuse to pay your debt I shall take you to court, and you'll suffer the disgrace of having your name bandied about – to say nothing of being committed to the debtor's prison and having your feet in the stocks."

"Take me to court?" Boccetta exclaimed with a laugh. "Well, go ahead! Or maybe you'd prefer to sit with your bare bottom on those stinging nettles over there? – the result might be less unpleasant for you. The debtor's prison? The stocks? O the infinite forbearance of God that allows a blockhead like you to live. Yes, go ahead and take me to court."

And with that Boccetta's face disappeared from the window.

Behaim found it difficult to reconcile himself even for a moment to this ignominious outcome. He found particularly galling the reference to stinging nettles; the remark seemed to him to have been meant seriously, for there was an abundance of stinging nettles in the garden that had run wild. He felt like smashing in the door so that he might have the satisfaction of battering Boccetta with his fists, but that would have been illegal and contrary to his nature; and besides, in contrast to the rest of the dilapidated house, the solid oak door was in good condition and not to be broken down with bare fists.

So there was nothing for it but to go away, and as he did so he applied to Boccetta and himself all the epithets that his fury suggested. He called Boccetta a scoundrelly, thievish and deceitful miser and himself an idiot, a blockhead and a good-for-nothing, who deserved a whipping, and he said these things to himself so loudly that passers-by turned and stared at him. He would like to see Boccetta rotting on the gallows, he declared, for God owed him that small satisfaction. And, having now included God in his list of debtors, he calmed down a little, for God, he had been taught, was on the whole a good and reliable payer, if sometimes a slow one, and He did not forget interest. And after this exasperating incident he felt he would be justified in treating himself to a jug of wine, that was something he owed himself. Therefore, as he took his obligations seriously, he went into an inn just inside the Vercelli gate, and the first thing he saw was Mancino sitting in a corner and thoughtfully gazing through the window at the busy street outside.

When Mancino looked up and saw Joachim Behaim his face reflected conflicting feelings. He was fed up with Behaim's endless questions about the girl he persisted in calling his Annie. But on this occasion his appearance on the scene was not wholly inconvenient, and he gave him a mixed reception.

"As my guardian angel has sent me you of all people, sit down," he said.

"That's no way to welcome me, sir" Behaim snapped. "I'm used to a friendlier reception and that's what I expect."

"You're quite right," Mancino admitted. "The first commandment is: Stay on good terms with those who have the money. So sit down and put up with my company. As for my guardian angel, he hasn't troubled about me very much in the course of my life, or I'd be better off and could offer you a young capon today or a breast of veal spiced with coriander."

"Don't worry about that," Behaim replied. "I only dropped in for a jug of wine."

"Hey, landlord," Mancino called out, "what are you prowling about for? A jug of wine for this gentleman. As you see, I don't lack friends."

He turned to Behaim, and went on: "My guardian angel shamefully neglected his duties towards me an hour ago when he allowed me to walk all unsuspecting into this inn. They seem to know me here, because, before you came, that fat hulk of a landlord didn't take his eyes off me for a moment; and that, even though to my own detriment I showed him a degree of consideration and forbearance that he doesn't deserve; I ordered nothing but a dish of swedes, and only managed to eat a third of it anyway. But never expect gratitude from an inn-keeper."

He fell silent, and a sad and remorseful expression appeared on his lined face.

"And why did you show him such consideration?" Behaim

asked quite unnecessarily, because he already knew the answer.

"Because he can see the moment coming when instead of getting paid he'll have my permission to feel my empty purse. And if he should then be dissatisfied and want to pick a quarrel, I'll give him a kick – or get one from him, depending on how fortune or the god of battles decides – after which I'll clear off as fast as I can."

"I shall enjoy that, it will be most entertaining," said Behaim. "But might it not perhaps also lead to a little knife-play?"

"That is quite possible," Mancino said gloomily.

"Well, I should very much like to see that," said Behaim. "But couldn't we perhaps first settle our little bit of business?"

"What business do you mean?"

"My guardian angel, who is not as unhelpful as yours but knows his duties," Behaim went on, "has put me in a position to order you a roast capon or spiced veal, whichever you prefer. You will then . . ."

"Hey, landlord," Mancino called out. "Come here and listen to what this gentleman says. Just listen to him, he speaks with the voice of the Almighty."

". . . you will then gain doubly," Behaim went on. "In the first place there will be the benefit to your soul of having done me a good deed by telling me where I can see my Annie again, and you will get the capon into the bargain."

"Go away," Mancino called out to the landlord, who had approached. "So it seems that I'm a person who will do anything for a meal. You're perfectly right, sir. Poor people, poor pay. And what am I in this world but a petty scrounger who sells what he has, sometimes verses, sometimes women. You're perfectly right, sir, that's what I am, you're perfectly right."

"So, if I understand you correctly, you agree to my proposal," Behaim said.

"Supposing I did so, I don't see what benefit it would be to you," said Mancino.

"Tell me where she lives and leave the rest to me," Behaim said.

"Take care," said Mancino, looking out into the street as if deep in thought. "Because of two bright eyes Samson lost the sight of his own. Because of two white breasts King David forgot the fear of God. Because of two slender legs the Baptist had his head cut off."

"Come, come," said the German with a laugh. "In this business I might perhaps suffer a dislocated ankle, but that's all."

"What might you suffer? I don't understand," Mancino said.

"I'll make my horse perform caracoles and curvets outside her house and get it to throw me gently. Then I'll call for help and groan and moan pitifully, and act as if I were unconscious, and they'll take me into the house. That's all I need."

"And what then?"

"Leave that to me," said Behaim, stroking his beard.

"Very well, then, you'll be lying in the street with an injured, dislocated or broken leg, and the only thing you can be sure of is that she won't let you into the house. Perhaps she might if you were a Frenchman or a Fleming, for Frenchmen and Flemings are in fashion, and the women of Milan regard them with favour. But Germans? They like them no better than Turks."

Behaim was offended.

"Don't be rude," he said.

"Perhaps after some time they might send for a barber-surgeon, who would patch up your leg," Mancino went on. "Consider whether you wouldn't do better to order the capon, which would bring you a double gain. In the first place it would be good for your soul, and also you'd still be sound in wind and limb."

"You might be right," Behaim admitted. "But it would be contrary to all commercial principles."

"Then keep the capon," Mancino said. "And if in spite of all commercial principles the generous idea of paying for my swedes occurs to you, don't imagine you will be doing me a favour. The landlord will be thankful for having got his money in that way. As for the girl, I knew she was going to pass this way and I was afraid you might see her . . . She did pass this way, and you didn't see her. You were busy making your horse perform caracoles in front of her house and then you were lying on the ground with a broken leg and looking the other way. So this time you've . . ."

He fell silent. The girl who was the subject of the proposed deal was standing in the inn. She was smiling, and gave Mancino a friendly nod. Then she came closer. Behaim sprang to his feet and gazed at her. She said:

"I saw you sitting here, sir, as I passed, and then it struck me that it would be a good opportunity to thank you for picking up the handkerchief I lost and returning it to me."

She stopped and took a deep breath.

"Oh, Niccola," Mancino exclaimed with anger and grief in his voice.

Joachim Behaim was lost for words.

Chapter 6

They met next morning in the church of Sant'Eusorgio; the encounter was brief but pregnant. They spoke to each other in the half-darkness behind a pillar, she whispering and he in an undertone, telling each other everything, the essential and the superfluous alike, with equal enthusiasm, in lovers' fashion. He wanted to know why, when they first met, she had not turned round even once, but had gone like the wind. She had several explanations for this. She had been confused, she did not know how he would take it, and in any case it was his business not to lose her from sight. And why did he call her his Annie when her name was Niccola? Anyway, he must lower his voice, because the woman kneeling in front of the wooden statue of St John had turned round twice already.

"But you must have noticed that I was in love with you from the moment I saw you, so much in love with you that I was nearly out of my mind," he said. "You must have noticed."

He had tried so hard to talk quietly that she had not heard anything he said. She smiled at him questioningly. He thought it necessary to describe to her in detail what had happened to him and in him, and he sought for the right words.

"It struck me like an arrow, it was so sudden, so painful and so unexpected," he explained in a whisper. "It struck me here, and it hurt, yes, deep inside me. But you walked on and left me, and that was wrong of you."

He paused, waiting for her to agree. But she had not heard this time either, for his voice was drowned by the footsteps of two monks pacing backwards and forwards. As he accompanied his words with an expressive gesture, pointing two fingers at his heart, Niccola guessed that he was talking about love, and she asked him whether there was anything special he saw in her.

"That's exactly what I'm trying to say," Behaim said so loudly that the woman praying in front of the statue of St John looked round at him for a third time. "I wandered about the streets every day looking for you," he said. "Yes, I'm crazy about you, and I behaved crazily."

What did he see in her, she wanted to know. There were much prettier girls than she in Milan, and much nicer ones too. And as she said this she briefly nestled up to him, as if to compensate for her remark. But the only word that Behaim heard because of her whispering was "Milan".

"Yes, it was only for your sake, only in the hope of seeing you again, that I stayed on in Milan," he said, and this was true, though until this moment he had refused to admit it. "You're the kind of girl that drives a man to distraction. I should have left long ago, I've no more business to do here. But there's just one thing."

His expression changed. The thought of Boccetta made cold fury rise in him. He gritted his teeth.

"I wish I could send him to the gallows," he muttered. "Perhaps I'll find someone who'll beat him to a pulp. But that wouldn't get me my ducats back; on the contrary, it would cost me money."

The girl saw his sour expression and the angry set of his mouth, and she could tell he had not been speaking words of love. He was angry, so she tried to pacify him.

"Perhaps it really was my fault," she said. "I could have walked a little more slowly. But I did drop my handkerchief. It wouldn't have been proper for me to do more than that, but in the end it really did bring us together, didn't it? And from now on you can see me every day, if you like."

He indicated that he had not heard what she had just whispered, and she repeated it rather more loudly.

"I said that if you like you can see me every day from now on. That is, if you really want to."

Behaim tried to seize her hand.

"Because of what you've just said I'd give you a hundred kisses straight away if we weren't in church," he said. "But as it is, damn it, I'll have to wait till we're outside."

She looked shocked.

"Outside in the street we must behave like strangers, as if we didn't know each other," she said. "We mustn't be seen together, it would be a disaster for me if I got talked about."

"Do you really mean that?" he asked. "In that case how are we to see each other in future? Listening to litanies here in church every day?"

She shook her head and smiled. She told him about a country inn that lay by a pond outside the city on the road to Monza; further on there was a small pine wood, where she would be waiting for him next day at about the fourth hour of the afternoon. Either there or, if the weather was bad – one had to think of everything – inside the inn. It was not more than half an hour away.

"That's nothing," Behaim assured her. "For your sake I'd tramp three or four hours every day. I'd climb walls, wade through ditches and defy snapping dogs in order to see you."

She smiled at him, and slipped away to a crucifix in a niche in the transept, where she bowed, crossed herself and knelt. When she came back a few minutes later she said:

"I prayed to Our Lord that there may be a happy outcome to our affair. So tomorrow at the fourth hour, you can't lose the way. I prayed for Mancino too. I have to tell you that he loves me, he loves me far more than you ever will. Now, of course, he's angry with me because of you and calls me unfaithful, but I've never given him any right to call me his. I prayed that he'll recover his memory and so be able to go back to his homeland. They say that once upon a time he was a great lord, with castles, servants, villages, woods and meadows. But he doesn't know where."

As she hurried away down the street she turned once and

smiled, holding up her hand and showing four fingers, to remind him of the fourth hour of the next afternoon.

In Milan there were two brothers of German origin, Anselm and Heinrich Simpach, merchants who had prospered from trading in the products of the Levant. Everyone knew them, for they had lived in Milan for twenty years, and it was to them that Behaim went for advice. They offered him wine, salted almonds and ginger nuts, and he wanted them to tell him what ways and means might exist under the duke's régime to force Boccetta to pay up.

Anselm was the older of the two brothers. He was a corpulent, sleepy-looking, rather ponderous man, and rising from his armchair to greet Behaim cost him quite an effort, while his brother was a restless, perpetually active individual who, whether he was standing, sitting, or pacing up and down the room, was perpetually fiddling with some object he had just picked up, whether it was a wine-glass, a wax candle, a medallion, a bunch of keys, a quill pen, or sometimes the hour-glass on the table, though this last always earned him a disapproving look from his brother. While Behaim expounded the facts of the case and the legal situation, which he did in detail and with great solemnity, and then went on to emphasize his determination to recover his seventeen ducats, the two brothers listened politely, though with ill-concealed indifference, and the elder brother did not always succeed in suppressing a yawn. But when he mentioned Boccetta their interest was roused and they started talking to Behaim with such animation that the sole object of each might have been to prevent the other from saying anything at all.

"But how is it possible, sir? Didn't you know that Boccetta . . .?"

"You should have known that about him, and that he . . ."

"He's mean, envious, full of lies and deceit," the younger brother interrupted the elder. "He's thievish, he's treacherous, he's a liar and he's crafty . . ."

"A base individual, without shame or honour," said the elder brother, "a person whom people like us keep well away from. Leave that hour-glass alone, Heinrich, it's quite all right where it is on the table. He's capable of any kind of villainy, though he comes of ancient and distinguished lineage. But his family disowned him long ago."

"Do you call him a person, Anselm?" the young brother exclaimed indignantly. "He's a monster, an abomination, a repulsive worm who succeeded in creeping into a human skin. I can't believe, Herr Behaim, that you had the misfortune . . ."

"I'm willing to do anything I can to help you. But with that Boccetta . . ." the elder brother interrupted the younger.

"Do you believe you're the first to have suffered loss because of him when he has spent his whole life . . ."

"Cheating and robbing people. He's one of those who don't fear the hand of God, because they don't realize how heavy and how close it is."

"Seventeen ducats, did you say? I'm surprised and delighted that you got away so cheaply, for he has only to look at a person to know how much he can get out of him."

As always when he was upset, Behaim rubbed his right arm with his left hand.

"He won't get anything out of me," he said resolutely. "He'll pay me those seventeen ducats, and he'll be weeping hot tears if he doesn't do so fast, because I shall take him to court."

The two brothers looked at him, one shaking his head and the other with a smile of commiseration. For a minute they said nothing, this time each of them seeming to want the other to do the talking; and with a dexterity that was surprising in view of his normal ponderousness, the elder brother took the glass dish of almonds from his restless brother just in time to prevent him from dropping it.

"Jesus, there was nearly an accident," he said. "What did you say? You want to take him to court? Boccetta? You're a stranger, what do you know about the administration of justice in this city?"

"Or about what litigation means here?" said the younger brother, looking about for a substitute for the glass dish.

"Particularly to someone who doesn't know the ropes here and is up against Boccetta." He produced a bunch of keys from his pocket, tossed it up in the air and caught it. "Are you really thinking of taking him to court? Then mark my words. It'll be you who'll weep hot tears."

"And that's quite apart from the appeals, objections, revisions and formal obstacles, of which there are dozens."

"To say nothing of the things that happen here, the mistakes, the spurious subpoenas, the documents that vanish and never reappear."

"You'll have to deal with assessors, expert witnesses, procurators, clerks of the court, court servants and messengers, every one of whom will want money from you . . ."

". . . and you'll find that you are continually and relentlessly having to pay, pay, pay. For drafting the summons, for revising it, for filing it, serving it, stamping it, for expert opinions on it, and for calling every single witness . . ."

"And you'll have to pay for permission to inspect the documents, for every single copy of all the documents required by the court, for every annotation made on the documents . . ."

"And for every registration, engrossment, signature, even every E and OE . . ."

"And one day you'll be astonished to find that your case has been dismissed *in absentia*. You'll make a fuss and apply for it to be reopened . . ."

". . . with that the whole thing will start all over again from the beginning," the younger brother added, "and you'll have spent all your money, and in the end, when you've tired of the whole thing and want to go away, you'll have so little left . . ."

". . . that you won't be able to afford a mule or a cart," the elder brother concluded, angrily putting the hour-glass out of his brother's reach.

"Is that the state of justice in the duchy?" Behaim exclaimed in dismay. "So that's why he told me to go and sit with my bare behind on his stinging nettles."

"Leave your behind out of it," the elder brother replied angrily, having heard only that one word and interpreted it his own way. "Am I responsible for the way justice is administered in these parts? I've only told you how things are here, and instead of thanking me for trying to keep you out of trouble, you get rude. It takes years for someone from over the mountains to learn the local customs and the way to go about things here."

"I beg your pardon," said Behaim, completely unable to understand the reason for the rebuke. "I didn't mean to offend you. I shan't go to court, then. But what am I to do? The idea of Boccetta's keeping those seventeen ducats from me out of sheer malice, and making me look a fool into the bargain, keeps me awake at night."

"If you can't sleep at night, try reading Holy Scripture," the elder brother suggested. "It will pass the time, your anger will subside, and sleepiness will take its place."

"A thousand thanks," Behaim replied. "But that won't get me back my seventeen ducats."

"Try to forget them," the younger brother said. "Try to put them out of your head. Wipe them out of your memory. Quarrelling with a thorough scoundrel like that whom decent people regard as beneath contempt, and for the sake of a mere seventeen ducats, is unworthy of a person like you."

"And don't worry about him," the older brother said. "He'll get his punishment in the next world."

"Of course, of course, I don't doubt that for a moment," Behaim replied. "But in this world I want my money."

"You don't seem to be open to advice in money matters. You're evidently stuck in your headstrong and obstinate ways."

"You should learn self-control and keep your greed in check," said the elder brother.

That was too much for Joachim Behaim.

"Enough of that, by the holy cross," he exclaimed. "You don't know me, and Boccetta doesn't know whom he's dealing with either, and he'll find out to his cost. So far everyone who has tried to take me on has been worsted."

The two brothers looked at each other, and the younger let out a whistle.

"If that's what you're thinking of . . ." he began.

"It would of course mean anticipating the divine judgment," the elder brother pointed out.

"But I don't know many people who would disapprove of a small foretaste of it being administered," said the younger one.

"Something of that sort, administered in the right dosage, of course, sometimes works wonders," the elder brother admitted.

"Increases willingness to pay."

"But you shouldn't undertake such a thing yourself. With all due respect to your skill and agility, you lack practice and experience. A little too far, and you'd find yourself in trouble."

"Also there's no need for you to do so. There are others who are available. You can find people who for a modest fee are willing . . ."

"You need only go to the Lamb, for instance, which is not far from the Cathedral, and ask for Mancino, or leave a message with one of his friends if he isn't there."

"He knows his job, he plants the knife as gently and neatly . . ."

"As any of us eats mackerel," the elder brother ended the lesson: and Behaim now remembered that at the Lamb, just when the wine was beginning to go to his head, Mancino had made him an offer of that or a similar kind. You have no need to trouble yourself, Mancino had said. Just leave it all to me.

Behaim rose to his feet and emptied his wine-glass.

"Thank you, gentlemen," he said. "That's a good idea, and the best thing about it is that it's easy to carry out. I know the Lamb, and I know Mancino. Normally I dislike doing anything illegal. But in this instance, as Boccetta's involved, it seems to me to be right and proper to adapt oneself to the customs of the country."

And with his hand he made the gesture of stabbing someone.

Chapter 7

When they met for the third time in the little pine wood on the road to Monza, they did not stay in the open but took refuge in the inn by the pond, for the sky was overcast and rain threatened. A buzzard chained to a block of wood greeted their approach by squawking loudly and beating its wings. Instead of the landlord and his wife, who were at work in the fields, a boy served the rare customers. In the cramped parlour he brought the girl milk and fig cake and Behaim a bottle-gourd of Friuli wine.

"He has been dumb from birth," the girl said when the boy left the room, "so he can't tell anyone I've been here with a strange man. That's a misfortune to him but an advantage to me, for only the dumb can be relied on. He's a relative of a priest in the neighbourhood, and people call him the nephew."

Meanwhile Behaim had tasted the wine.

"I don't want you to complain one day that I've concealed the truth about myself from you," he said, "so I'm telling you now that when the wine's good I'm capable of swallowing a horse and carriage. And this one strikes me as not at all bad."

"As you didn't use a horse and carriage to come and meet me here, drink as much as you like," she answered.

In their lovers' talk they kept coming back to their first encounter in the Via San Jacopo and the amazing miracle of their having met again in a vast and populous city.

"I had to find you," Behaim told her, "because you made me fall in love with you at first sight, and so deeply that I couldn't have gone on living unless I saw you again. But you didn't do anything to help me to find you."

"What should I have done?" Niccola wanted to know.

"You never went back to the street where we first saw each other," he complained. "I looked for you there often enough. I even left my inn, which had every comfort and convenience I needed, and moved into a miserable house in the Via San Jacopo in order to keep a better watch for you. I sat at the window for hours hoping to spot you among the passers-by."

"Did you really want to see me again as much as all that?" Niccola asked.

"What a question," Behaim replied. "You know very well that you have only to look at a man to drive him out of his mind."

"Are you saying that someone has to be out of his mind to want to see me again?" Niccola asked. "That's a strange thing to say."

"Oh, stop it and don't muddle things, you know very well what I mean," said Behaim. "You looked at me, made me mad about you, and made off as fast as your legs would carry you, leaving me stranded and completely at a loss what to do. And believe me, I'd have risked eternal damnation to find you again."

"You shouldn't say things like that," said Niccola, crossing herself.

"And if I did meet you again, it was due to the sheer chance that led me to the inn where Mancino was sitting and waiting for you. You did nothing to help."

"Didn't I?" said Niccola, smiling and blushing. "And now Mancino's angry with me. I haven't seen him since, he keeps out of my way."

"You did practically nothing to help," Behaim insisted. "You were looking for Mancino, not me."

"You saw me passing by, but didn't think of hurrying after me," Niccola said. "You saw me, and just sat there and let me go. I remember, you had a jug of wine in front of you, and you weren't willing to abandon it for my sake. So much for your keenness to see me again. And what did I do? I saw you sitting there with Mancino and said to myself: Stop, Niccola, if this isn't an opportunity . . ."

This was just what Behaim wanted to hear, but he didn't admit it, he wanted more of the same from her, so he went on:

"So you saw me sitting with Mancino. And what did you see in me?"

"Well, I looked at you, and looked at you again, and basically I didn't really see in you anything I disliked."

"Well, yes, I'm not lame or hunchbacked, and I don't squint," said Behaim, stroking his chin, cheeks and beard.

"And I said to myself: Niccola, you know that in matters of love it's sometimes the woman who has to take the initiative. But whether it was the right thing to do in this instance . . ."

"There's not the slightest doubt about that, you did exactly the right thing," said Behaim. "You know the state I'm in, you know that I'm nearly out of my mind because of you."

"So you've told me," said Niccola, "and perhaps you're really in love with me, but only in moderation, as a great lord and nobleman loves a poor girl."

As she said this she looked out at the pond and the trees all round it that seemed to be trembling under the downpour, and some of the melancholy of the landscape crept into her soul.

"It would be crazy of me to hope for more than that," she went on.

"I'm no nobleman," Behaim exclaimed. "I'm a merchant, I deal in one thing and another, and that's how I make a living. Here in Milan I've sold two horses, and I'm living on the proceeds for a while. Also . . ." and his face darkened when he thought of Boccetta, "I have debts to collect."

"Thank heaven," the girl said. "I thought you were a nobleman. I thought you were a nobleman belonging to a great family. But I much prefer it as it is. Because it's not a good thing in a love affair if one party eats cake and the other nothing but a little millet gruel."

"What do you mean?" asked Behaim who, as he had been thinking about Boccetta, had been listening with only half an ear. "Do you call me millet gruel because I don't belong to the nobility?"

"I'm millet gruel and you're cake," Niccola explained.

"What? You millet gruel? What are you talking about?" Behaim exclaimed, and stopped thinking about Boccetta. "You know very well that you're the loveliest girl in Milan, you just want me to tell you all over again that I love you to distraction and there's no one like you anywhere."

Niccola flushed with pleasure.

"So you're fond of me? You like me?" she said.

"How did you manage it?" Behaim asked. "Did you put forget-me-not in my wine or my soup? When I'm not with you I can't think about anything but you. I've never been so much in love in all my life."

"That's good," said Niccola. "I'm glad."

"And what about you? Do you love me?" said Behaim.

"Yes," Niccola said. "Very much."

"Say it again."

"I love you very much. I love you very much indeed."

"And what will you do to prove it, to show me that it's true?"

"Does it need any proof? You know it's true."

"The first time we met you promised me a kiss, and very much more," said Behaim.

"Did I do that?" Niccola said.

"Your eyes did," said Behaim. "There was a promise in your eyes. And now I want you to keep it."

"I shall be delighted to let you kiss me," Niccola promised. "But not here, where that young man, the nephew – no, please, not now, stop it, listen to me. Why didn't you yesterday, when I was with you . . ."

She wanted to remind him that he had not kissed her the day before, when they had been alone and undisturbed in the little pine wood, but she couldn't say anything, for he had decided the right moment had come and had drawn her to him, and while she yielded to his embrace she managed to keep her eye on the door and the window and at the same time listen to the nephew's footsteps as he went down to the wine cellar.

Quite a time passed before Behaim let her go.

"Well," he said, "what is my beloved doing?"

"She sends you her best wishes," said Niccola, making an attractive little bow. "And the saying one hears so often, that a kissed mouth loses nothing, may well be right. It renews itself like the moon."

And she licked her lips like a cat that has been drinking milk.

"Do you mean you've never been kissed before?" Behaim wanted to know.

"You don't have to know everything," said Niccola. "Perhaps I'm the sort of girl that lets herself be kissed at every street corner."

"But you ought to know," said Behaim, "and I'm telling you now, so that it won't lead to any argument later, that I'm not one of those who are satisfied with kisses only."

"So I've noticed," said Niccola, trying hard to introduce a note of severe rebuke into her voice. "While you were kissing me you also allowed your hands to wander. That was most improper. And I certainly haven't promised you that after so short a time . . ."

She stopped, for just at that moment the boy who was serving them walked in with a jug of wine. She flushed with embarrassment, for she didn't know how much he had heard. She went to the window and looked out at the road and the pond. The rain had stopped. The buzzard ruffled its feathers and sharpened its beak on its chain.

She talked to herself, quietly and without moving her lips. Perhaps it's true that he loves me, for he's not one who makes fine phrases, she said to herself. Yes, I think he loves me. But he has loved many women before me. God help me, and may what has developed between us have a happy and joyful ending for me, for how could I keep from You, and You know Yourself, that I shall be his if he wants me.

On that rainy afternoon Messer Leonardo went, as he often did, to the bird market that was held twice weekly near the Porta Nuova. While wandering among the stalls, booths, tents and barrows, looking at the birds in their prisons or dungeons made of osier switches or dogwood branches, he questioned the sellers about how they caught the birds, whether by whistles, limed branches or nets; he also listened to their complaints about the tremendous care and patience that their calling required, in spite of which it was very poorly rewarded.

For a half scudo that had unexpectedly landed in his pocket that morning Messer Leonardo bought several siskins, two thrushes, two chaffinches and a woodpecker which, as was his custom, he wanted to set free in a meadow or wood outside the city. For he enjoyed watching the different ways in which birds behaved when they were released after a long time in confinement. Some fluttered about uncertainly, as if they did not know what to do with their liberty, while others flew up and away and quickly vanished from sight.

He set off along the road to Monza with some friends, one of whom, Matteo Bandello, who in spite of his youth had already gained a reputation as a story-teller, carried the birdcage. He had come to Milan from Brescia the day before for the sole purpose of finding out how far Messer Leonardo had got with his *Last Supper*.

"I wish," he said to the court poet Bellincioli, with whom he was walking, "I wish I could put into the story I'm now working on, which I propose to call *Portrait with Many Meanings*, only a fraction of the multiplicity of forms and their inter-connections that Messer Leonardo puts into all his pictures. And that wealth and abundance is the more remarkable when one takes into account how recent is the practice of this art in our age, for until the time of Giotto it lay buried under the stupidity of mankind."

"You wrongly praise the little I have so far done in painting, Matteo," Leonardo said. "It may well be that I learnt something in Florence from Master Verrocchio, whose pupil I was, just as he may have picked up one or two things from me. But it was only here in Milan that I became a painter with this *Last Supper*."

"And that's why what you'd like best," Bellincioli said with a trace of irony, "would be to be allowed to spend the rest of your life on that *Last Supper* and continue with your experiments with paint and varnish."

"There's nothing I want more than to finish it," Leonardo replied. "Because I want to be able to devote myself exclusively to the study of mathematics, for it is in mathematics that God's counsels are clearly discernible. But for this *Last Supper* I need heavenly as well as earthly aid if it is to be something great that will live for all eternity and bear witness to me. It's true that for some time now I haven't been on good terms with my brushes and paints, but two or three years are not long for a job like this. Also you must take into account that I am a painter and not a pack-ass. And even if I don't pick up my brush every day, I spend two hours every day in front of the painting, thinking where to put the figures, what form, posture and air to give them. To say nothing of the hard work in the streets, taverns and elsewhere, which incidentally earned me a half scudo this morning. To me it was more than welcome, for without it I should not have been able to buy freedom for the little prisoners that Matteo is carrying on his back."

Messer Leonardo was asked what the story behind this half scudo was, so he explained: "You know that this picture, in which I show our Saviour sitting at table with his disciples, has called for a great deal of unforeseen work that takes up a great deal of my time. Sometimes I'm struck by someone's chin, forehead, hair or beard, and I follow him all day long wherever he goes, so that I can study his character and personality and base Jacob or Simon Peter or another of the twelve disciples on him. And this morning I was following someone in this way when he turned and approached me angrily and said: 'Here's your half scudo, you damned nuisance, and for your information I found it in the gutter, and now clear off and don't trouble me any longer, and take better care of your money in future.' And off he went, and I watched him talking angrily to himself for some time. And that, gentlemen, is how I acquired the half scudo, and it's all the money I had, for yesterday, I gave my servant Giacomo, whom you call Greedy Guts, cloth for a new coat and cap in order to have some peace at last, because he was at me all the time with demands and complaints."

"And now you've spent your money on that good-for-nothing thief and liar, a man who steals your bed linen to use as kindling in the stove, you've found nothing better to do with your half scudo than to take it straight to the bird market," said the woodcarver Simoni, who was walking behind Messer Leonardo with Marco d'Oggiono.

Bandello stopped and turned his cheerful, boyish face to the woodcarver, whom he had made a butt of his jokes ever since he first met him. "So you didn't know, Master Simoni," the writer said as he walked on beside him, "that Messer Leonardo is busy with the problem of bird-flight? Very soon he'll have solved it, and all these little creatures, finches and siskins and the like with which I'm burdened, will have helped him. Your role in this is of course bigger and more important than mine, and I can see the day coming when I'll find you lying in hospital, where your . . ."

"In hospital? Me?" the woodcarver interrupted.

"Yes, with several fractures of the arms and legs as a natural consequence of the experiment. But you'll be famous. We're all consumed with envy because, if Messer Leonardo gets his way, you'll enjoy the honour and distinction of being the first mortal to rise to the clouds on eagles' wings – just like a god."

"Eagles' wings?" exclaimed Marco d'Oggiono. "That has by no means been decided on yet. All that Messer Leonardo has mentioned to me is that he has decided on a pair of bats' wings for Master Simoni. Of course you surely know that bats' wings are much cheaper than eagles' wings."

"What is all this?' the woodcarver cried in dismay. "Heavens above, doesn't Messer Leonardo know I'm in the middle of working on my *Ecce Homo*? And doesn't he know that in these hard times I also have to keep my father, who is old and ill and can't work at his trade any longer? Me up in the clouds? And without even asking me? What an idea. Is the old man, ill as he is, to beg in the street? And you" – he turned violently on young Bandello – "a young fop and good-for-nothing with no responsibility for anyone . . ."

"But consider, Master Simoni," Bandello interrupted him. "You are used to and practised in working the hardest wood with hammer and chisel. Your biceps must be far stronger than most people's. That's why Messer Leonardo has picked you for the job, and not me, because I use nothing but a pen. So accept the situation. I do my bit too. I'm carrying a whole cageful of thrushes, finches and siskins all this way on my back without a murmur, simply to help Messer Leonardo. Talk to him, Master Simoni, and don't be bashful. Tell him you insist on the eagles' wings you're entitled to, not those wretched bats' wings, which are unworthy of you. Go and talk to him right away."

He pointed to Messer Leonardo, who had increased his pace and was now waiting with Bellincioli in front of the inn by the pond, where Niccola and Joachim Behaim were engaged in their courting.

The painter d'Oggiono put his arm round the woodcarver's shoulders and acted as if he had some excellent advice for him.

"Now take care," he said. "With bats' wings you wouldn't come to any harm. They wouldn't take you up to the clouds; you'd hover just over ground level, and if you fell all you'd get would be a fright, and perhaps a broken leg. You could finish your *Ecce Homo*, and you'd still be able to carry on your trade, indeed with a much enhanced reputation and, if you walked with a limp or dragged one foot a little, nobody would notice. So listen to me and not to Bandello, for what I'm telling you is for your own benefit. Hurry up, go and talk to Messer Leonardo, and insist on bats' wings."

The woodcarver looked in bewilderment and despair at d'Oggiono, who kept a straight face, and he was just about to hurry ahead to talk to Messer Leonardo when his eyes fell on Bandello. The writer could contain himself no longer and had burst out laughing, and Simoni realized they had been pulling his leg. His relief that the dangerous prospect had been averted did not prevent him from losing his temper, and he began to curse and swear.

"Go to the devil, you sons of whores, and may he tear out your wicked tongues," he declared. He called down on them the plague, the pox, bone decay and every other kind of affliction, and expressed the hope that the very air they breathed might be accursed. "I didn't believe a word you said from the start," he added. "It's not so easy to fool me."

With this, he wiped from his brow the cold sweat that the fear of death had put him in.

Outside the inn by the pond Messer Leonardo was meanwhile explaining to the court poet Bellincioli how essential it was for a painter to know all about the anatomy of the nerves, muscles and veins.

"In the enormous variety of human movements and in every expenditure of human energy," he said, "one must be able to recognize which muscles are being used, and one must emphasize those muscles alone, and not all the others. And those who cannot do this should paint bunches of radishes and not the human form."

He turned to the others who had arrived by now and said:

"We shan't stay here. You, Matteo, will have to carry your burden a little farther – I forgot about this disturber of the peace." He pointed to the chained buzzard, which was fluttering about and squawking excitedly.

"Yes, we'd better go on," said Bandello. "He scents the birds I'm carrying, and his squawks are frightening them to death. None of them will leave their prison while this predator's about."

They went on towards the pine wood. The woodcarver stayed behind, looking back at the inn. Then he caught up with the others.

"She's gone, she won't appear again," he reported. "She appeared at the window for only a second, but I recognized her . . ."

"Whom did you recognize?" asked d'Oggiono.

"The girl Niccola," the woodcarver replied. "You know,

the money-lender's daughter. And, though she never even glances at me, I'm always delighted to see her, she's so charming. She goes to Mass at Sant' Eusorgio."

"Yes, she's beautiful," said Messer Leonardo. "God performed a great miracle when he made her face."

"She comes from Florence, and she has the light ethereal walk of Florentine women," said the woodcarver.

"But," the poet Bellincioli pointed out, "neither her ethereal walk nor her beauty has got her a husband or a lover."

"What? A lover?" young Bandello called out. "Haven't you noticed that Master Simoni here is head over heels in love with her? Do you deny it, Master Simoni? Go back and talk to her. Tell her what you feel about her."

"Talk to her?" said the woodcarver, taken aback. "You think that's so easy?"

"Go, and don't be so timid," the boy Bandello said to him. "You're a handsome fellow, you'll find she's no prude. Or would you like me to try? It's only a matter of finding the right thing to say."

He acted as if he were confronting the girl and, in spite of the bird-cage on his back, he managed to produce a very elegant bow.

"Signorina," he began, "if I have not arrived at an inconvenient moment . . . No, that sounds too ordinary. Let me start again. My beautiful signorina, as I have had the good fortune to meet you so unexpectedly, I ask you as sincerely as I can to accept my love and to tell me how to gain yours . . . What do you think of that, Master Simoni? Do you like it? Now that's something you can't buy at the apothecary's."

"Leave her alone," said Bellincioli. "She knows better than to get involved with the likes of you. She's well aware that she'd end up mocked and jilted. Believe me, it's no joke being as beautiful as that if one happens to be Boccetta's daughter."

They walked on in silence for a while.

"I tell you she has a lover and she's with him now," d'Oggiono said suddenly. "And he must be a stranger in this city, someone who doesn't know who her father is. So this is where she meets him. I should like to know whether . . ." He shrugged his shoulders and said no more on the subject.

"They've gone," said Niccola, going back to Joachim Behaim's arms with a sigh of relief. "It was Messer Leonardo and his friends. Some of them would certainly have recognized me. What a horrid fright. If they'd seen me – God bless my soul, nothing worse could possibly have happened to me."

Chapter 8

When Joachim Behaim told her that for the sake of seeing her again he had moved into a cheap attic room, the sole advantage of which was that it looked out on to the Via San Jacopo, thus enabling him to see the precise spot where he had first set eyes on her, she decided immediately that nothing would stop her from seizing the first opportunity of going to see him in his miserable attic, if for no other reason than to see where and how her beloved was living. The idea that this might get herself talked about no longer worried her, for by now she was so much in love that caution took second place. But as Behaim, instead of inviting her, went prattling on about his endless hours at the window vainly waiting to catch sight of her, she realized that she would have to take the matter into her own hands.

"I hope you don't imagine I might come and see you up in that room, whether it's a good one or bad one," she said, smiling up at him. "You know how wrong it would be, and so you won't ask it of me. I don't deny there are plenty of women in this city who would be delighted to do it, but I'm not one of them, as you know. It wouldn't be decent, and even if I brought myself to do such a thing for your sake because you wanted it so much, tell me honestly: what would your people at home think of me? Perhaps you might be able to manage things so that no one living in the house ever saw me; but has it occurred to you that if you left the door open for me I might easily be seen slipping in by someone who knew me? What then? My goodness, that's something I'd rather not think about. It would be the end of my reputation, and the whole town would start pointing its finger at me. So we'd better not mention the subject again, don't you agree? If you have the slightest regard for my reputation, you must try to put the idea right out of your head."

Behaim morosely rubbed his left arm with his right hand. His displeasure was directed at himself, and he called himself an idiot for not having broached the subject in the right way. He was well aware, of course, that he had never made the proposal that Niccola objected to so strongly, but he was convinced that he must have betrayed his thoughts and wishes by some premature and ill-considered remark that had spoilt the whole thing.

"Of course," the girl went on after some reflection, "you may be right in thinking we're no longer safe from prying eyes here in this inn. That has occurred to me too. First there was Messer Leonardo passing with his friends a few days ago, and yesterday, as I told you, I passed someone on the way here who stared at me – I can't tell you how – as if he knew all about us. That worries me. You don't think I could come without being seen and without running the slightest risk, perhaps with a handkerchief over my face, do you? A lot of good that would do. People are always telling me they can recognize me a mile off by the way I walk. Tell me, darling, do you see anything distinctive in my walk? You don't? Or do you? Really? And you think I might risk it in spite of that? That would take a great deal of courage, which I don't have. But there must be some saint for a poor girl to appeal to when she wants to go unseen to her lover's house. There's a saint for each human undertaking. When I was a child I was told to implore St Catherine to help me learn to read and write. Then I learnt singing and playing the lute with the aid of St Cecilia, as well as how to spin wool, because that is how I wanted to earn my living, though I enjoyed making coloured paper flowers much more, because I'm very good with my scissors. So tell me, darling: should I light a candle to St Catherine before coming to see you, or would St Jacob perhaps be better in this case, as the street is dedicated to him? It would be best of all if I could rely on the saint who helps thieves to enter people's houses unobserved, but I don't know his name. Mancino could help me there, because he knows everything and everybody connected with thieving, but he's been angry with me for days."

When, to the accompaniment of kisses and assurances of love, they had decided on the day and the hour and all the other details, Niccola, with a quick glance round the room at the tavern that had now served its purpose, bade it farewell and slipped out. Her lover stood at the window and watched her go, feeling very pleased with himself at a success which he attributed to himself alone. From the road she raised her arm in the failing twilight and showed him three fingers to remind him to expect her at the third hour of the next afternoon.

As he had to ensure that she should remain unseen by inquisitive eyes when she arrived and crept up to his room next day, Behaim decided that it would be advisable once more to take the candle-dealer into his confidence. He found him frying chestnuts and apples for his supper on the kitchen stove.

"Come in, come in," he called out, delighted at the prospect of having someone to talk to. He greeted Behaim by brandishing over his head the wooden spoon with which he was stirring the chestnuts, as if it were a sword. "I bet you've come to invite yourself to my supper, you can smell the apples cooking all over the house, and these chestnuts are the best to be had in the market, they come from Brescia. There's enough for two, it won't take a moment to lay the table, and I can also offer you a fine salad. Today you'll be my guest, and tomorrow I'll be yours. So sit down and set to."

And, as having a good meal at someone else's expense was in his view one of the greatest pleasures in life, he went on: "If you like, I'll tell you straight away what my favourite dish is, so that you'll have plenty of time to get it ready for tomorrow. What do you say to a sucking pig for the two of us?"

Behaim, rubbing his left arm, said: "I came to tell you that tomorrow . . ."

". . . is a fast day?" the candle-dealer interrupted. "Yes, I know. On that point I'm no better than a Turk. I don't mind eating a sucking pig – or a partridge, if you prefer it – on a Friday, and if you say it's a sin, it's one that can be easily washed away in a little holy water. Or, if you like, we can keep the fast like good Christians by having a ragout of tenches, or even better, shrimps fried in butter with fried bread, that's a proper supper for a fast day." And he tilted back his head, shut his eyes, and acted as if he were relishing the taste of the shrimps on his tongue as he swallowed them one after another.

"We'll certainly have supper together one day, if not today or tomorrow," Behaim said. "But today I only came to tell you I'm expecting a visitor tomorrow. She has done me a great honour by accepting my invitation to come and see me here."

"Who's coming here?" the candle-dealer asked without any special curiosity; and, having awoken from dreaming about his favourite dish, he peeled two chestnuts and popped them in his mouth.

"The girl I was after. I've found her," said Behaim.

"I don't know whom you were after. Whom have you found?" asked the candle-dealer.

"The girl," Behaim said. "The girl I told you about. Don't you remember?"

"So you've found her. Well I'm not a bit surprised," said the candle-dealer. "Didn't I tell you you'd find her? I even told you where to look for her. All you had to do was to follow my advice. You see the trouble I take to help you, as you're a stranger here and not very clever and totally inexperienced into the bargain. And, now that you've found her thanks to the hints I gave you, are you still as much in love with her?"

"Yes, now I've got to know her, I love her even more than I did before," Behaim admitted.

"She must be a very attractive young creature if you're to be believed," said the candle-dealer. "Well, I shan't keep my advice from you. Take her and enjoy yourself with her, keep her for a few days but not too long, and then pass her over to me and find yourself another one."

"Why the devil should I do that?" Behaim exclaimed in surprise. "You know how I dote on her."

"That's just why I'm giving you this advice," said the candle-dealer. "One day you'll be grateful and shake me by the hand for it, because I'm talking to you as a friend. I can tell she's the sort that needs neither fife nor drum to make men dance to her tune. If you get too involved with her, you'll soon be quite at the end of your tether, and that's when you'll find you're stuck with her."

"So I'm to get rid of her?"

"Yes, get rid of her gracefully and in good time."

"What are you talking about?" Behaim exclaimed. "Kindly note that the only idea in my head is to do everything to keep her. I'm certainly in no hurry to end this affair, and that's why when I leave here I'm determined to take her with me, for she's the loveliest and cleverest and best woman I've ever met, and there are not many things on this earth that mean so much to me as being in love with her."

He did not pause for breath until he had told the candle-dealer precisely how matters stood.

"Love," said the candle-dealer with a deep sigh. "What do you know about it? Brief pleasure and long, bitter tears, that's what love is, unless you care to call it a mere figment of the imagination that disturbs one's senses, which is what the philosophers call it. So you imagine you love her, and you're determined to keep her for yourself. Hell, it would be stupid to try to do a good turn to a person who cannot appreciate it. So let us not discuss the matter any further. Anyway, what about that other person you asked me about? Has he paid you back the money he borrowed from you?"

"Don't talk to me about him," said Behaim with mounting anger. "He'll pay up, you can be sure of that. I'll have him begging me to accept the seventeen ducats he owes."

"It occurs to me," said the candle-dealer, attending once more to the apples on the stove, "that perhaps your young lady has a friend of her own sex, an attractive young person like herself, for these girls often go in pairs. If she brought her friend along, I should have no objection, because when there's a foursome the talk is far livelier than when it's only a threesome."

"Threesome? Foursome?" Behaim exclaimed indignantly. "What are you talking about? There's no question of a threesome or a foursome, I want to be alone with her and stay alone with her, and that's that. Do I make myself clear?"

"No, you don't," said the candle-dealer. "Why do you want to deprive her of the pleasure of enjoying my company too? You can take it from me, it's worthwhile being in my company when I'm in the right mood. When I'm in high spirits, everything I say is witty, I quite bubble over, and everyone's creased up laughing."

"Now you listen to me," said Behaim, seething. "I expect her tomorrow at the third hour in the afternoon, and I promised her she wouldn't see a single strange face in this house. So my advice to you is to keep out of the way. If you show yourself even for a split second I'll give you such a hiding that the doctors will spend weeks discussing how to get you back into a state when you're just able to crawl again. You see, that's the sort of person I am. Now do you understand me?"

"As you wish, as you wish," replied the candle-dealer, more startled than hurt. "I'll shut myself up in my shop as yet another act of pure friendship for you. Threats won't get you anywhere with me, but if I'm approached in the right way I'm willing to do anything to oblige. Besides, there was something else I was going to tell you. You know the price of wheat is rising, wine is getting dearer, and I've had to buy four loads of wood, this winter's been so severe. And my bladder complaint has been troubling me. So you'll understand if I increase your rent by two carlini a week. What you're paying me now doesn't even pay for my supper."

She slipped into her clothes with quick, supple movements, and when he tried to put his arms round her and lovingly draw her to him again she eluded him, for it was late. She took her leave for that day with a comic little grimace, turning down the corners of her mouth and rolling her eyes. In the doorway she held up her fingers to indicate the time he was to expect her next day. She used the same fingers to blow him a kiss, and then she left him.

She crept quickly down the stairs. In the hall she heard a door creak and through a chink she saw the flickering light of a candle. She could not find her handkerchief, which she must have left upstairs with her lover, so she raised her arm and hid her face behind it as if behind a protective mask; then she was through the door and out in the Via San Jacopo.

Up in his room all Behaim's thoughts were on her and the hour that had just passed.

Now she's mine, he rejoiced, she loves me, and obviously I'm the first to whom she has given herself. What a beauty she is. Now I know how beautiful she really is, and she's so sweet – what a lucky devil I am. She loves me, and isn't that a great blessing granted me by God? And she's coming here again tomorrow. Damn it, tomorrow I must have something to offer her, sweets, fruit juice, cakes – fancy not thinking of it today. I'm smitten with her, that's obvious. I'm in such a state, I don't know whether it's heaven or hell. It's heaven, except that when she's not with me I have no peace, it's hell. She's coming again tomorrow. If only it could stay like that, if only I could say every day that she'll be with me tomorrow. Now we really know each other – but what's the good of saying that, the world, or life, will part us again. If only I could keep her. May God have mercy on me, what a life I've been leading all these years. Here, there and everywhere, on horseback or at sea, now with the Greeks, now with the Turks, now with the Muscovites, and then back to the warehouses in Venice. Then off again, to markets and courts, always after accursed money. God help me, what sort of ideas are these? Am I nothing but a lover, then? Am I not a merchant, a man of the scales and the yardstick? I no longer recognize myself, I'm a changed man. What maze have I wandered into?

He went to the window, opened the shutters, and let the evening air blow round his brow.

She's my darling, he said to himself, why shouldn't I keep her for ever by making her my wife? Do I want wealth, country estates, a splendid town house from her? She's beautiful and clever, well mannered, modest, and she loves me – what more do I want?

He withdrew from the window. He was amazed that the idea of marrying her and taking her with him when he left Milan had not occurred to him before. Now that he had made up his mind a great peace came over him. Everything seemed simple and straightforward.

What do I need if I'm to marry her? he said to himself. It's easy enough. All that's necessary is a priest and two witnesses, and that she should say yes, and that's all.

On her way home in the twilight Niccola went into the church of Sant' Eusorgio to talk with God about love and her lover.

"Perhaps You are angry," she said softly, kneeling before the statue of the Saviour, "perhaps You are angry that I have given myself to him without Your holy sacrament. But wasn't it You that put into my heart the desire that drove me into his arms every day? It happened this afternoon. True, I didn't keep him waiting long, but I said to myself that, when two people love each other as we do, they should lose no time, for nobody knows what the morrow may bring. If I've done wrong, don't make me pay for it. Look mercifully on our love, guide it so that it may lead to his happiness and mine."

Her father bolted the door at the same time every evening, even when she was not yet home, so that she had to knock and shout before she was allowed in, and then, when at last he let her in, she had to listen to his scolding; so she stayed only long enough to say a quick Lord's Prayer.

Outside the church door stood the woodcarver Simoni; he was in leather apron and clogs and carried his chisel in his hand as he had come straight from work and had hurried across the road to be present at the Elevation of the Sacred Host. The sight of Niccola made him stroke his moustache with pleasure, and he raised the cap from his bald pate in greeting. She thanked him with a fleeting smile and went on her way.

I don't know him, but he greets me whenever he sees me, she said to herself as she hurried along. He looks at me as if he knows where I live. Is he perhaps one of those who have pledged something to raise some cash? No, he doesn't look as if he's in my father's hands. Oh, how ashamed I feel when people give me that pitying look. Little do they know that I earn my own living with the work of my hands. Mancino knows, he sometimes brings me wool to spin. I hope I don't meet him today. He looks me in the face and knows at once where I've been and what I've been doing. He mustn't find out. He loves me, and if he knew what has happened he'd burn out like a candle.

The door was not bolted. As she went up the rotting wooden stairs to her bedroom she heard Boccetta's voice from below.

"Stop talking about God's mercy and Christ's suffering, it's as useless as blowing at a cold stove. Ill, did you say? He can be as ill as he likes, and he can die if it gives him any pleasure, it doesn't matter to me. You stood guarantor for him, and you'll pay. And now be off with you, sir, go with God or go to the devil, as you please. You will bring me the money tomorrow. Otherwise I shall have the pleasure of seeing your head sticking out between the bars of the debtor's prison."

Upstairs Niccola flung herself on her bed.

Darling, she muttered, take me with you. Take me away from the strange man who is my father, take me away from this house, which is worse than a prison, take me away from Milan. You ask whether I shall love you always. Take me with you, darling, and if in the next life there's love like earthly love, I'll be yours for all eternity.

The candle-dealer, who had watched her through a chink tripping lightly out of the house, closed the door and blew out the candle to save money.

She's beautiful, he admitted to himself. Tall and slender. That German is one of those who always pick the best. I've had enough of him. He comes down to the kitchen, talks a whole lot of nonsense, and wastes my time. But she loves him, she loves him dearly. That's what girls are like nowadays, they take no notice of us and run shamelessly after foreigners, they're rotten to the core. They behave as if they were pious and respectable, but in their hearts they're guilty of all seven deadly sins.

Chapter 9

On the evening when Behaim went again to the Lamb no friendly fire was burning in the hearth, and the place was meagrely lit by two smouldering oil lamps which hung from the smoke-blackened ceiling among the sausages and strings of onions. When Behaim looked about him he recognized the bald-headed man with the moustache who had described himself as the novice master of the inn, as well as several young painters and artisans in whose company he had got dead drunk that evening. Also the man in friar's habit who was said to teach mathematics at Pavia University was sitting at his table with a chalk in his hand, immersed in contemplation of his geometrical figures. But there was no sign of Mancino. Behaim was anxious to talk to him; this was the second time he had come here for the sole purpose of doing so, though he had pleasant memories of the wine the landlord had served him with on the previous occasion. Then he had not even known Niccola's name, and now she was his mistress, and he had made up his mind to marry her and take her with him wherever he went, so now there was nothing to keep him in Milan – except for the little matter of Boccetta and the seventeen ducats he was determined to recover, and for that purpose he needed the help of someone who could handle a cudgel or, if necessary, a dagger.

When he asked the landlord about Mancino, the man grimaced as if he had bitten on something hard and lost a tooth on it, and laughed a short and bitter laugh.

"Mancino?" he exclaimed. "Are you looking for him here today? And do you expect to see His Most Serene Highness the Duke and his Eminence the Cardinal Archbishop of Milan in my house? A ducat, sir, is a goodly sum of money, it will take him several days to get through it, that is, unless he surrounds himself with a dozen loose women who set about carousing at his expense. But you're quite right, he's perfectly capable of doing just that, for that's the sort of person he is."

"I didn't ask you about the archbishop," Behaim answered irritably, "and I don't care how many loose women Mancino associates with or how he enjoys himself with them. I asked you where he is."

"Don't you know?" the landlord said in surprise. "Well, you're a stranger, that accounts for it. When there's money clinking in Mancino's pocket, he's to be found in any of the other taverns or bars in this city, in the Crane or the Bell or the Weaver's Shuttle or the Mulberry Tree, and he won't show his face here again until he's spent his last three-copper piece. Then he'll turn up here again, you can be sure of that. Landlord, he'll call out, bring me something to drink on tick. Be a Christian, landlord, and think of your immortal soul. That's the sort of person he is, and the rest of them are no different, whether they're painters or stone-masons or organists or poets. If you know one of them, you know them all, and that one over there in monk's habit is just the same, he has been sitting there for weeks without producing half a quattrino from his purse, using up my chalk and spoiling the table top with his scrawling – yes, it's you we're talking about, reverend brother, I was just telling this gentleman, who was asking about you, how clever you are with your books and how learned you are – yes, that's what they're all like. And I, sir? If I have anything to reproach myself with, it's my excessive kindness of heart. As you know, sir, I'm of a peaceable disposition and very patient, but I'm not going to put up with these people much longer, you can be sure of that."

Behaim interrupted the landlord's tale of woe.

"So you think he's come into some money?" he said.

"All my customers know it," said the landlord. "He was seen in the Bell yesterday changing a ducat, dozens of people have told me that. A ducat, sir. Would you believe it? Mancino!

He's said to have had it from Messer Bellincioli, who is a poet too, but is a great lord in the service of His Most Serene Highness. They say he got it for some verses he handed over to Messer Bellincioli by order of the ducal household. But do you believe that? A ducat for a few verses? If it was for knifing someone, he's a master at that, it might be credible. But for a few verses? The idea makes me roar with laughter. If it were really true that one could earn good, solid ducats by writing verse, I'd be writing verse instead of standing here serving dunces and simpletons with my good Friuli wine. Yes, sir, that's what I'd be doing. And now, sir, what can I get you? A jug of my Vino Santo from Castiglione, praised by everyone who has ever tasted it?"

When Behaim had the wine jug and pewter mug in front of him and began appreciatively sipping his Vino Santo, his enjoyment was accompanied by increasing fatigue, and as he sat there resting his head on his hand, sipping the wine and wondering how many days it would be before that cut-throat and tavern poet Mancino had drunk his ducat, confused snatches of the artisans' and artists' talk at the tables all round him came to his ears:

"What times these are. Nowadays nobody's willing to spend even a quattrino in honour of God and the Virgin Mary."

"Before I could even begin I needed a little blue paint. So I told him . . ."

"He can't do much, flowers, vegetables and small animals are what he's best at. But, fool that he is, he got it into his head that . . ."

"I should have listened to my father and become a cook in a cook shop, because for a well cooked meal . . ."

"Whenever I see her in the street, I always stop and look at her, even if I'm in a hurry, I can't help it."

"Reverend brother, I'm no theologian, but you know nothing about painting, so you can't say . . ."

"He wants to paint the life of his patron saint on eight great big panels . . . puts it down to the call of honour – the silly ass!"

"Just to get started at last, I told him to go and buy an ounce of the best varnish he could obtain in Milan."

"Mathematics permeates and illuminates human life, and as a mathematician I know . . ."

"My father said I'd never be able either to clothe or feed myself on what I earned from art."

"As a mathematician you can't possibly know how difficult it is to paint the shift of an eye, or its lustre."

"To me what you are saying sounds presumptuous. Give music its due, but don't call it a sister to painting."

"And if the best-quality varnish is unobtainable here, I told him not to bother, but to bring me back the half carlino."

"I saw her today too, and I watched her for a long time, but what good does that do me?"

"Stupid as he is, he now regards himself as the beacon of Italian art, and there's no talking him out of it, more fool he."

"Talk to her? If only it was as simple as that. And besides, look at me, bald and fat as I am, what a dreary lover I should make. To say nothing of my age."

"Because painting doesn't die almost as soon as it's born the way music does. It gloriously and magnificently survives . . ."

"Yes, ever since I was a boy I've never wanted to be anything but a painter . . ."

"I see her every day, generally outside the church where she goes to Mass."

". . . and survives, not just as a faint memory, but as a living thing."

". . . and that's unfortunately what I became."

"A living thing? That's ridiculous. All I see is an application of mixed paints and some varnish."

"There's Mancino. He's turned up just at the right moment. As you cling to your error as stubbornly as a mule, let him decide between us. He's neither an organist nor a painter, but when he recites his verses he's as close to music as he is to painting. Hey, Mancino!"

When Behaim heard the name of the man he had been waiting for so impatiently, he started out of the drowsiness to which he had succumbed, less from the wine he had drunk than owing to the confused and sleep-inducing buzz of conversation going on all round him. He looked about him. Mancino was standing in the doorway, swaying slightly as if he were a little tipsy, and he waved to the two young men who were inviting him to join them at their table. Behaim rose. Mancino had begun wandering round the room, stopping momentarily to exchange a few words here and there with friends. Behaim approached him and addressed him with a politeness bordering on deference.

"I wish you every good fortune, sir," he began. "I have been waiting for you, and, if it is not inconvenient, I should very much like to have a few words with you."

Mancino looked at him irritably. It was impossible to tell whether he regarded Behaim as a successful rival or merely as a bore and nuisance to be got rid of as quickly as possible.

"Then tell me what is on your mind, sir," he said after a moment's reflection, and he made a gesture towards the two young men who had chosen him to adjudicate in their dispute about whether painting or music enjoyed primacy in the arts – they would, he indicated, have to wait.

"In the first place," Behaim said, "I should like you to join me at my table and to be my guest if you have not yet had your evening meal."

"Alas," Mancino exclaimed, "I was born under an unlucky star. The invitation with which you have honoured me comes too late, sir, for an hour ago I satisfied my appetite with an excess of bread and cheese. That such a thing should happen to me shows that I am out of favour with the Almighty. But should that surprise me? Me, who goes through life with such a heavy load of sin?"

"That," said Behaim, thinking of the cheese rather than of the heavy load of sin, "need not prevent you from joining me in emptying a jug or two of the Vino Santo that the landlord serves here."

"You have just said something," said Mancino, taking his seat at Behaim's table, "that is capable of making even a completely desperate man, even one damned to the blackest depths of hell, oblivious to his fate. Hey, landlord, don't hang back, come here, and take this gentleman's order. But you," he said turning back to Behaim, "certainly didn't wait for me here simply to treat me to Vino Santo."

"I have been given your name," Behaim explained, "and you have been highly recommended to me, as a man who can be confidently and dependably relied on in difficult cases. Your health, sir."

"And yours," Mancino replied. "Yes, there are those who have that opinion of me, though there are others who think it time I retired from business and left it to others because, they say, I'm not much more than the stump of a flickering candle likely to be extinguished by a breath of wind. However that may be, I am at your service."

"It's strange," Behaim said reflectively, "but now that I'm sitting facing you I have the feeling, or rather I'm almost certain, that I once saw you years ago. Your face is not one that is easily forgotten. I was sitting over a glass of wine outside an inn at which I was staying somewhere in Burgundy or Provence. It was a summer's day, and I saw a procession coming along the street; there were two pikemen on the right and two on the left, and in the middle was a man they were taking to the gallows, and that man was you. But, so far from looking like an evil-doer, you walked proudly, head up, as if you had been invited to dine at the duke's table."

"In my dreams I often see myself on the gallows, with a fat priest offering me a silver cross to kiss," Mancino calmly replied. "But you didn't come here to listen to my dreams. Oblige me by telling me what you want of me."

"For a skilful, intelligent and experienced man like you, what I want you to do will not be difficult," said Behaim.

"It may be difficult or even dangerous," said Mancino, "and it may even be . . ." he lowered his voice to a whisper . . . "contrary to the laws of the duchy. All that does not frighten me. All it depends on is the degree of generosity shown me, for, as you know, I'm not blessed with earthly goods. True, in the next few days I shall have very little time to spare, for any amount of work is waiting for me, but if we come to terms – you know what it says in the Bible: one must be ready to leave one's boat and one's nets for a good cause."

"Then let us come to the point," said Behaim rather more quietly. "I have been told that that dagger of yours" – he glared at the weapon in Mancino's belt – "is a great miracle-worker that has sometimes taught a stubborn individual to see reason."

"That's true," said Mancino, and his hand glided lovingly over the leather sheath of his dagger. "It could long since have obtained its master's or doctor's degree in the art."

"So that leaves me with nothing to do but to look around for some monks who would be willing to pray for the salvation of his soul."

"The salvation of his soul? You underrate me, sir," Mancino said. "Stubborn though this person may be, you should not be after his life. There are of course people in my business whose knives do not observe a proper degree of moderation. They stab and kill like the bunglers that they are, and the result is nothing but trouble. No, sir, I'm not one of them. My dagger practises moderation."

"So you think that milder action, say a blow in his damned face, might be sufficient to persuade the rogue to . . ."

"Yes, I could manage something of the sort," said Mancino. "It would be something appropriate. You can depend on it. You would be completely satisfied."

"Very well, then," said Behaim. "Deal with him as you think best, though I should prefer to see Boccetta hanged, with his tongue hanging out of his mouth."

For a moment there was silence. Mancino raised his head and looked at Behaim. He had raised his pewter jug to his mouth, but he put it back on the table, leaving the wine untouched.

"So when you give him what is coming to him," Behaim went on, "don't go about it too gingerly. Take into account what Boccetta has done to me and many others. Take care, but at the same time make sure he'll have good cause to remember me."

Mancino stared straight ahead of him and remained silent.

"So you know what I want," Behaim went on, "and I think we're in agreement so far as Boccetta is concerned. All that remains is for you to let me know your fee. I know that a job of this kind is not done solely for the love of God. So tell me what it will cost."

Mancino remained silent.

"Name your price," Behaim went on, "and let me know how much you want in advance in return for all your trouble. You will receive the rest when the job has been done to my satisfaction. You can rest assured that I am a punctual payer, and I can give you the names of persons of repute in this city who will confirm it."

Mancino sighed, shook his head, brushed his hair away from his forehead, and broke his silence.

"As I mentioned at the beginning," he said, "I have no time at present for a transaction of this sort. I have to think about my own business, which is important to me, because there's no one who can do it for me."

Behaim thought Mancino was merely trying to put up his price, and that annoyed him.

"Stop beating about the bush and name your price," he said. "It's no use making a long rigmarole about it; that won't get you anywhere, so come to the point. You'll do all the better out of me that way."

"I'm afraid it's no use, you've approached me for nothing," said Mancino, looking worried. "I can't help you, sir, for a matter like this, with its special circumstances, needs careful preparation, for which I have no time. Also I'm by no means as sure of my touch as I used to be, and that might easily result in difficulties for both of us."

"Let me make it quite clear," said Behaim. "Your advance will be paid out to you at this table straight away, as soon as we've come to terms."

Mancino made a dismissive gesture with his hand.

"I understand you perfectly well, but you don't seem to understand me," he said. "I can't help you, and I've told you why. You must also bear in mind that Boccetta is an old man, and setting myself on him would bring me little credit."

"Is it credit you're after?" Behaim asked excitedly. "Aren't you interested in the money to be earned, and so easily earned, in this matter?"

"Let someone else worry about the money," Mancino replied. "I'm not interested in it. So don't let us discuss it any further, it would be a waste of time. And now if you will excuse me . . ."

"What on earth has come over you?" cried Behaim in dismay. "A few minutes ago you were talking quite reasonably, and now you want to let me down. You know how important the matter is to me. What am I to do to get back the ducats that rogue is keeping from me illegally?"

"If you want my advice," said Mancino, rising to his feet, "what I say is this: Take your time, wait and see how things develop, and don't do anything in a hurry. Today's one day and tomorrow's another. If today you've lost money to Boccetta, tomorrow you'll get it back from someone else."

"Damnation," Behaim exclaimed angrily. "That's enough of your rubbish. One moment you say he's going to get what's coming to him, and that I can rely on you; and now, when it comes to the point and it's a matter of using your dagger in a good cause, you're frightened, are you?"

"Maybe," said Mancino. "That's the sort of person I am."

"You're a coward and a braggart. With you it's nothing but words. You're nothing but a Frenchman whose shirt doesn't cover his backside, a charlatan and a windbag."

"All right, you can call me that if it gives you any pleasure," Mancino replied. "And now you've said your piece, be off with you. Yes, sir, that's the best thing you can do, clear out of here as quickly as possible, or there may be no holding me."

He put his left hand on the hilt of his dagger and with his right pointed imperiously to the door. Meanwhile customers at neighbouring tables had noticed that a quarrel was breaking out, and Simoni the woodcarver stood up to restore peace.

"Hey, you two, which of you is causing trouble?" he called out.

"Has that German got drunk again?" one of the stone-masons wanted to know.

Mancino made a dismissive gesture, as if the affair was of no account.

"Everyone has his own devil to torment him, and his has put the idea in his head that it's his duty to turn Boccetta into a man of honour."

"Honour?" Behaim shouted furiously. "Who's talking about honour? I want my seventeen ducats back."

All round him there were roars of laughter and much shaking of heads, and the painter d'Oggiono was the most amused of them all.

"So it's about those seventeen ducats, is it?" he called out. "And what about our bet? Is that still on? You bet me two ducats to one."

"Yes, the bet still stands," Behaim said sulkily.

"In that case the two ducats are as good as in my pocket already. You Germans are well known for keeping your word."

"Yes, we keep our word," Behaim said loudly and emphatically, for Mancino's benefit, as Mancino had gone and joined the organist Martegli at his table and was talking to him with total unconcern. "But don't count your chickens before they're hatched. I don't know how the matter may end up so far as Boccetta's life and limbs are concerned, but there's no doubt whatever about my getting my seventeen ducats back, because I know myself. So you're the one who'll have to pay up."

"Seventeen ducats from Boccetta?" Brother Luca said with a sigh, without looking up from the table top on which he had chalked and proved an algebraic theorem. "How do you suppose that such a thing might be possible, sir? If Boccetta could save his father from purgatory by paying half a scudo, he wouldn't do it."

"What I don't understand," said the stone-mason, "is that at a time when Christendom is being devastated by the plague and there is a threat of war, you are able to worry your head about such trifles."

"You call it a trifle that I want my money back?" Behaim

shouted angrily. "You must imagine I stole the money."

"Take my advice," said Alfonso Sebastiani, a young noble who had left his estate in Romagna to become Messer Leonardo's pupil. "Go to bed early, eat light food, sleep a great deal and as long as you can, and then perhaps you'll see your money in dream."

"Spare me your nonsense, sir, it annoys me," Behaim snapped at him. "I'll get my money back, even if I have to break every bone in Boccetta's body one at a time."

"Well," said d'Oggiono, turning to him full of curiosity but not without a trace of irony, "what will your young lady say if you do that to him?"

"My young lady? What do you know about my young lady? I have not told you who my young lady in Milan is. Whom are you talking about?"

"About Niccola; she is your young lady. Haven't you been seen every day waiting for her at that peasants' tavern on the road to Monza? And doesn't she come hurrying to you like a young doe every day in her one good dress?"

Behaim leapt to his feet and looked furiously about him as if he were surrounded by mortal enemies.

"How dare you meddle in my affairs, sir?" he said, rounding on d'Oggiono. "What concern is it of yours if she's my young lady? And if she is, she'll get all the fine clothes she could ask for, just leave that to me. What the devil has any of this got to do with Boccetta, I should like to know."

This time it was d'Oggiono's turn to be astonished.

"How can you ask that?" he exclaimed. "Don't you know, or are you only pretending not to know, that she's Boccetta's daughter?"

"Oh!" cried Simoni, stung with jealousy. "Niccola, the moneylender's daughter – is he her lover, with whom she . . . Is she this German's mistress?"

Behaim glared at them like a boar cornered by hounds.

"What are you saying? Have you both gone mad?" he shouted. But he knew already with deadly certainty that they were speaking the truth, and it was like a stab to the heart.

Chapter 10

In anguish, desperation and fury, Joachim Behaim wandered about aimlessly until daybreak, his head in a spin. The narrow, dark streets led him right across the city to the encircling wall with the Naviglio canal and St Eustace's Cross, where hedges and garden walls began. Beyond stood the gates of the new poor-house, from the windows of which there came the smell of fresh bread, which was baked there nightly at Il Moro's expense. Then he wandered all the way back until at last he came to the fish market and passed the money changers' stalls and reached the town hall and finally the Cathedral square. He sat on the steps leading up to the door of the Cathedral. In spite of his exhaustion he could not rest, and after a few moments he resumed his disconsolate wandering.

What dreadful news that was, the worst imaginable, he said to himself as he walked on. Job himself suffered nothing worse. What wickedness, what deceit, what treachery. She looked so frank and ingenuous, she acted as if she were devoted to me, she was all smiles, she talked about anything and everything, but kept to herself the fact that she was that infamous rogue's daughter. What a scoundrel he is, and what a disaster that I fell in with her. That bald-headed fellow at the inn, the one with the moustache, called her the moneylender's daughter, that doesn't sound so bad; but Boccetta's daughter sounds quite different, like a smack in the face. What a fool I've been to fall into such a trap. Why did I allow myself to be carried away by this treacherous love? Where will it lead me? She told me her mother was a Lucardesi. Yes, her mother. But her father is

Boccetta, and that she kept from me – may he go to hell and take her with him.

He stopped, and pressed his hand to his hammering heart. In his agitated mind the angry thought now took on substance, he imagined he could see Niccola falling into the flames of hell and disappearing in the glow. He was terrified as he thought he could hear her agonized shrieks mounting from the abyss, and he realized with intolerable anguish that he still loved her.

That voice of hers, he groaned as he went on his way, how it touches my heart. If only I could forget it, banish it permanently from my ears. But if a hundred voices spoke to me and one of them were hers, it would be hers alone that I would hear. O God, O merciful God, let me forget her voice, let me forget everything that drew and bound me to her. Take away the memory of her voice, her walk, her eyes, her kisses, her smile – O merciful God, let me forget that she can smile as only an angel can. You know she's Boccetta's daughter. Hear me, O Lord, and set me free, let me forget her for ever, or release me from life itself, for that's what I'd prefer.

After speaking to God and appealing so urgently for His aid, he felt a little better, and he tried hard to view what had happened to him in a different light.

What has in fact happened? he asked himself. A slight mishap that might occur to anyone, an irritating episode about which there's little to be said – that's all it amounts to. I was a bit infatuated, I let my head be turned by that young thing. That's bad, certainly, but these things happen, and now that I've found out who she is and where she comes from, thank heaven – it's all over, it must be all over. The fact of the matter is that it would be against all reason if I remained in love with Boccetta's daughter, it would be ridiculous. Love? Can that be called love? No, it was no more than an ill-considered lust that got the better of me, and I'm well on the way to recovery.

But the consolation he tried hard to get from these words did not last long. A loving phrase that Niccola had whispered in his ear during their embraces occurred to him, and her image immediately appeared in his mind's eye. He saw her lying by his side in all her beauty, snuggling close to him, willing and determined to be his. He remembered the unforgettable moment when he had recognized that all the world's wonders were but rubbish in comparison with the pleasure he enjoyed in her arms, but instead of the joy and rapture of that moment he felt pain, shame, grief and despair breaking over him like a flood.

It's not true, it's all lies, he silently shouted at himself. Why do I lie to myself? How can I get over it, it's too difficult, she'll always be there, how can I forget her? That's the state I'm in, I couldn't be more wretched, oh, how I despise myself. She's Boccetta's daughter, and I know she is. I can't shake her off, I can't turn my mind to other things, to business, markets, rising prices, the goods waiting for me in the warehouses of Venice. What lunacy possesses me, so that all I can think of is sleeping in her arms, on her breast? Where does this leave my honour and my pride? Is it possible to live in such torment and to love a woman whom one should not love? Was I to know she was born to sow mischief and bring me unhappiness and disgrace? May God punish me, but I'd rather have the daughter of an unwashed peasant as my mistress. Accursed be the hour when I met her. What business had I to be in the Via San Jacopo at that moment? Mancino was singing in the market place, and it was his fault that I ran after her. I saw a girl, I thought her beautiful and charming, and she smiled at me. I lost her from sight, perhaps my guardian angel had something to do with that. And, fool that I was, I got it into my head that I must find her, I searched for her everywhere, I didn't give up, I found her, she became mine, and then – look what happened to me. What am I to do now? I can't remain in love with Boccetta's daughter. Is such a misfortune to be borne? The devil himself would sympathize with me if he knew my situation.

He put his hand to his brow and felt the cold sweat on it, and he shuddered.

I'm ill, he groaned, I feel like death, I'm shivering with cold, I ought to be back in my room. A jug of mulled wine spiced with stonecrop would do me good. I'm feverish, it's getting me down and confusing my mind. Perhaps all this is only a feverish dream, perhaps it isn't true and I'm only dreaming, and she isn't his daughter. No, alas, I'm not dreaming, I'm in my right mind, I know what has happened to me, and I'm wandering about the streets. I ought to be at home.

It was morning when he reached his lodging and went up to his room. He flung himself on the bed and lay there, oppressed by tormenting thoughts, until a restless sleep took pity on him.

The day was well advanced when he awoke. For a time he lay there in a haze, unable to think clearly. He knew that a misfortune had happened to him and that he had been suffering, but he could not tell what it was. He felt terrible, and he knew he was confronted with something that frightened him. Then memory of the previous evening returned, and d'Oggiono's voice rang in his ear, saying: "But don't you know she's Boccetta's daughter?"

The memory overwhelmed him like a paralysing shock. A moment later, however, something else struck him with overwhelming force and made him see his predicament in quite a different light.

Is it so certain that they were speaking the truth? he asked himself. Isn't it more likely that those two men in the Lamb, that d'Oggiono and that other man, thought up a wicked joke to make me look a fool? What they told me was pure invention, a brazen lie, and I fell for it.

This idea surprised and delighted him, and he got up and paced up and down the room, completely cheerful again.

No, it isn't true, it can't be, they told me a brazen lie. Out of youthful high spirits, no, out of sheer malice. I'll remember it and get even with them. Niccola, Boccetta's daughter? What an absurd idea. Her nature is so utterly different, she's a pure soul, she doesn't care about money or possessions, she wouldn't accept the smallest present from me, wouldn't even let me buy her a belt, or one of those small embroidered purses in which Milanese woman keep their silver coins. Boccetta's daughter? What a thing to try and put across me.

He stopped and recovered his breath. Now that his heart felt lighter and his agitation was subsiding, he felt a need to talk to others instead of to himself and to hear what they had to say about the stupid trick that had been played on him.

His landlord the candle-dealer was not alone. With him in the kitchen, which smelled of fried bacon, was the neighbourhood cobbler, a wrinkled old man with a sparse goatee beard. He had repaired the worn soles of the candle-dealer's best pair of shoes, and after much haggling had at last agreed on the price for the job; and the candle-dealer had very reluctantly and to the accompaniment of many protests paid out six quattrini on the kitchen table.

"A blessed day, may God grant you good fortune," Behaim said by way of greeting as he walked into the kitchen. "Have I come at an inconvenient moment? If not, I must tell you about the strangest things that have been happening to me."

"This gentleman," the candle-dealer explained to the cobbler, "lives in my house and often comes to see me and ask my advice, because what would he do without me? For he is a stranger, and everyone in the city is out to diddle him."

"I'm an honest man, I'm well known in the neighbourhood, and I don't diddle anyone," the cobbler said to Behaim with his hand on his heart. "If you have shoes to mend, you as a stranger will not have to pay more than is the custom."

"In heaven's name," Behaim said to the candle-dealer without taking any notice of the cobbler, "you've no idea how true what you've just said is. A real attempt has been made to deceive me. Two men have been trying to persuade me that my girl, the one I told you about, is Boccetta's daughter."

"Boccetta's daughter?" the candle-dealer exclaimed with every appearance of surprise. "Really? Would you ever believe it?"

Then, after thinking it over for a moment, he asked: "Who is this Boccetta, anyway?"

"What? You don't know him?" Behaim exclaimed in surprise. "I thought everyone knew him, because he swindles and defrauds everyone. I've told you all about him. He's the man who refuses to pay me the seventeen ducats he has owed me for years. Of all the thievish usurers in this city he's the worst. A man without shame or honour."

"She may be his daughter or somebody else's," said the candle-dealer. "She's a tasty morsel. Anyone who has her for the night is in clover. She's just right, not too plump and not too skinny. The only thing I don't like about her is that she runs after strangers. She's too good for the likes of us Milanese."

"Have you seen her, then?" Behaim asked.

"She ran into me once or twice on the way out after leaving your room," said the candle-dealer.

"Didn't I promise you I'd thrash you black and blue with my belt if you caught sight of her even once while she was in the house?" Behaim said angrily.

"He's joking," the candle-dealer explained to the cobbler. "This is just one of his jokes. Actually he and I are the best of friends." He turned to Behaim and went on: "So you say she's the daughter of that thievish usurer?"

"That's what d'Oggiono says; he's one of the painters I met at the Lamb. But I don't believe him. He's a lying busybody."

"I told you that you'd have nothing but trouble with those people," the candle-dealer said reproachfully. "You can't say I didn't warn you. But did you take any notice of me? No. You wouldn't listen to me. You would go and squander your money in the Lamb, and in return they served you with nothing but lies. You should have stayed at home and let me cook your meals, for I'm well known in the neighbourhood for my good cooking."

To demonstrate the validity of this claim he took a pan from the fire in the hearth and invited both Behaim and the cobbler to taste the lentils he had cooked with bacon for his lunch.

"No, you shouldn't call d'Oggiono a liar," the cobbler said after he had tasted the lentils and put the spoon aside and licked his lips. "You're mistaken about that, sir. Messer d'Oggiono sticks meticulously to the truth." Then he told the candle-dealer what he thought of his cooking.

"At home I use less vinegar, and put in two or three thin

slices of apple and some thyme, and that improves the flavour."

The reference to slices of apple and thyme upset the candle-dealer.

"Everyone does as he thinks best," he said sharply.

"You mentioned d'Oggiono," Behaim said to the cobbler. "Do you know him?"

"Yes, he's the one who painted the *Madonna in the Clouds* that hangs beneath the big window in the ambulatory of the Cathedral choir, I know him," the cobbler replied. "He has brought his shoes to my shop for years. He has two pairs, one of sheepskin and the other of Cordovan leather that he wears on feast days. And when he has no money, he says: Master Matteo, you must be patient with me, I can't pay you today, write down that I owe you eight quattrini, or nine, or ten, or whatever it may be, write it down, he says, and on Friday I'll come and pay you. And, when he says that, it's as if he had taken an oath on the Holy Scriptures, and he turns up punctually with the money. D'Oggiono's no liar. You can trust him, I tell you, he sticks to the truth."

This cast a cloud of unease over Behaim.

"In that case the girl, Niccola, would be Boccetta's daughter," he said.

"I don't know, and I don't care," the candle-dealer said crossly. "She's your girl and not mine, don't forget. And I've told you several times what to think of girls of that kind. And, just at the time when everyone is sitting down to lunch, do I have to listen to all this talk about this female and whose daughter she is, and about slices of apple and Cordovan shoes, and heaven knows what besides? You have had your money, Master Matteo, what I have to pay I pay, and here nothing needs to be written down, so goodbye, Master Matteo, goodbye."

Behaim too said goodbye, and he left the kitchen and the house in a state of complete uncertainty about whether or not to believe what d'Oggiono had said. But if he was speaking the truth, he said to himself, when he was outside in the street, and if I really have had the misfortune to make that rogue's daughter my mistress, I know where she lives, and all I have to do is to watch the house, and if I see her coming out, which heaven forbid – O God, let me wait outside the house for nothing and waste my time. But if I see her coming out of his house I know what I have to do. But do I know? Am I sure of my own mind? Shall I be able to overcome my desire? Shall I be able to listen to reason and do or not do what reason prescribes? Or shall I be unable to stop loving the girl?

And with an uneasy heart he set out for Boccetta's house.

Chapter 11

Mancino did not have so much as a copper coin that would have enabled him to buy a slice of barley bread for his lunch. He was therefore in a thoroughly bad mood when he made his way through the dense undergrowth of the derelict garden behind the back of the house by the well. He stopped under Niccola's window. She might well have been at home, spinning wool or mending her dress or otherwise busy in her room, for the shutters were open to let in the meagre light of that dull and rainy day.

He had not come for Niccola's sake. He wanted a word with Boccetta, but there was time for that, it could wait. He stood there, lost in contemplation of the cracks and fissures in the walls of the dilapidated house, and noted that there were plenty of footholds for anyone who wanted to climb in, and he said to himself that it would not be impossible, in fact it would not be very difficult, to climb up to Niccola's window and land in her room and in her arms. Even though the shutters were closed and barred at night, the wood was rotten and would yield to a powerful blow.

When he caught himself pursuing this idea he grew furious with himself, and shame came over him, together with melancholy.

Look at you and what you are, he began his self-denunciation. Do you still call yourself a scholar? You're a loafer, a pauper, a fool and a clown. You're a stable boy, handy with a knife when occasion arises, chained all your life to this abject poverty; and now you're in the winter of your life, and how long will it be before they carry you away and pronounce over you the ritual words, *De terre vient, en terre tourne*? How did I come to lose my youth? How and when did it happen? It stole away like a thief in the night, and suddenly I saw that it had gone. And now, fool that you are, you want to climb up to Niccola's room and beg a little love from her? I wish I could kick you, you fool, so hard that you'd land on your backside, because that's what you deserve. Didn't you swear, when you were still in your right mind, never again to approach her with the stale, pitiful and shallow feeling you call love? But now you're at it again, for you won't listen to reason. In love? You're making a fool of yourself. You'd find love as painful as the goad which drives the ass to its work. What do you expect with your face, which is no longer a face but a grimace, with dull, sunken eyes and cheeks wrinkled like a worn out, discarded leather glove. That's what you're like, and you want love from her, though you know she doesn't want you and belongs to someone else. You have no pride, you're worse, you're more despicable than a rat. Clear out from here, stupid brute and idiot that you are.

Having made his feelings plain in this way, he fought his way through the undergrowth round to the front of the house without another glance at Niccola's window. There was no need to knock at the door, for Boccetta was at his barred window, listening to a mendicant friar asking for alms in honour of the Holy Trinity while the miser displayed his unpleasant features to him and to Mancino and to anyone else who passed the house.

He shook his head sadly, as if he were sorry that someone had played a dirty trick on this poor friar. "Someone has deliberately and maliciously directed you to the wrong house," he said, "for everyone knows that nobody gets any alms here."

The friar knew by experience that it was rare for anyone to give alms at the first time of asking. People in the city had to be reminded two or three times that they were in this world only on a short lease, and that their time in purgatory could be reduced by good works.

"Give, sir," he said to Boccetta, "give for the sake of God's mercy and the merits of the blessed saint who was the founder of our order. Your donation will be to your benefit, for God keeps His eye on all who honour Him by acts of charity. Grace comes from God."

"Yes," said Boccetta, catching sight of Mancino and casting an amused glance at him. "Everyone knows that – just as everyone knows that Cremona's the place for hot sausages."

"Just a small donation," the friar went on undeterred. "One day it will serve you as a signpost when you reach the crossroads in the next world. It's not much that I ask of you. A little cheese, an egg, a little fat, for, as the saying is, alms and Masses wipe away sin."

"You amaze me, good brother," said Boccetta. "Fat, cheese, an egg? You expect a real feast from me. Have you not considered that, in addition to all the other suffering that God imposed on sinful mortals, He included hunger in their inheritance? In seeking to deprive humanity of that inheritance you are acting contrary to the will of God. I ask you, is that right? Is it Christian?"

"What you have said is very learned theology, and I am only an ignorant friar," replied the mendicant, bewildered by this unexpected argument. "But I do know that we are in this world to help one another in our tribulations. What else are we in the world for?"

"To help one another?" Boccetta exclaimed, bursting into loud laughter. "What an idea. No, good brother, helping others is not in my nature, I'm not made that way, and besides, it's generally associated with useless expense and extravagance. If you've understood me, good brother, go and knock at someone else's door."

The friar was by now completely intimidated and had almost given up hope, but he made one last attempt to obtain alms from Boccetta.

"Consider," he said, "that God created man to be good and to do good works."

"What did you say?" Boccetta exclaimed. "To be good and to do good works? Stop, unless you want me to laugh myself to death. To be good and to do good works? That's too much, stop it, my jaw's aching already."

The friar picked up his alms bag and hoisted it over his shoulder.

"Farewell, sir," he called out. "May God in His mercy enlighten you, for it seems you are in need of light."

He went, and when he came to where Mancino was standing, he nodded to him familiarly, stopped and said: "If you have anything to ask him, may God grant you more patience and better luck. I talked the soul out of my body. He won't take a quattrino from his pocket, even for the faith, it's unbelievable."

"He can't see anything good in anyone in the world, and that includes himself. A pig would turn up its nose at the bread he eats," Mancino replied.

"Hey, you!" Boccetta called out to Mancino as the friar walked away shaking his head. "If you've come to do business, you can save yourself the trouble, it won't do you any good. You can abuse me and swear at me as much as you like, I don't take any notice."

"I came to give you a warning," Mancino said. "Take care, you're in danger, it looks as if there's going to be murder. That German's after you."

"What German?" Boccetta calmly asked, and then seemed to think hard for a moment. "The devil take me if I know what you're talking about."

"Wasn't there someone who wanted some ducats from you which you refused to let him have?"

"Oh, him? You mean him, do you?" Boccetta said. "Now I remember him. As a punishment for his sins he must have got it into his head to ask me for ten or I don't know how many ducats. He came here and made a nuisance of himself. He wouldn't talk about anything but those ducats, and I had a lot of trouble getting rid of him."

"Then just take good care of yourself," said Mancino, "because that German regards your refusal as a disgrace and a scandal, and he's in such a towering rage I shouldn't put anything past him."

Boccetta smiled a lop-sided ironic grin, and remained completely unruffled.

"Let him come," he said. "I'm quite ready to receive him. Some people go to do some fleecing but come back shorn."

"I know," said Mancino, "that you're an old hand at dirty tricks, and that you know a hundred ways of keeping money that comes your way even if it isn't yours . . ."

"You flatter me," Boccetta interrupted. "You make too much of the modest abilities that God granted me."

"But that German knows his way around; he's looking for someone, and if he finds the right man to give you the *quietus* with a knife or axe . . ."

"Let him come," said Boccetta. "It's a game at which two can play."

"But isn't the German in the right? Don't you really owe him the money he wants from you?"

Boccetta rubbed his stubbly chin and looked surprised, as if that were the last criticism he expected.

"In the right? What do you mean by that?" he replied. "He may be in the right. But what does that matter if I don't feel in the mood for charity and wasting good money on an idiot?"

Mancino looked up at the face behind the bars without speaking for a moment. Then he said: "You are a nobleman. You come of a great and illustrious family that has more than once provided the city of Florence with its gonfaloniere, who carries the banner of justice – tell me why you live this shameless and dishonourable life?"

For the first time something like annoyance and impatience appeared in Boccetta's expression.

"Dishonourable?" he replied. "What do you know about honour? I'll tell you something you should note, and note carefully. He who has the money has the honour. And now, if you have anything else to say to me, say it, and don't bother me any more with that fool of a German."

"Very well, I shall go," said Mancino. "I've warned you, and it wasn't out of any love for you, I assure you. So now, if you're stabbed, or slashed across the face from ear to ear, it's perfectly all right with me."

And he turned and left the garden.

"Let him come!" Boccetta yelled after him. "Just let him show himself here. Tell him he won't see so much as a three-copper piece, not a three-copper piece will he see, tell him that, and then come and tell me what he croaks in his fury."

He let out a laugh that sounded like a hoarse bark, and his face vanished from the window.

Joachim Behaim was hiding behind some bushes by the garden wall, his eyes fixed on the front door, waiting for Niccola to appear like an inescapable blow of fate. He had overheard Boccetta's remarks and realized that it was to him he was referring and that it was he who was not to see so much as a three-copper piece out of the money owing to him. Hot fury rose in him, the veins on his brow swelled and his hands trembled.

Just as well I heard that, he said to himself. Good heavens, was there ever such a villainous rogue? Not a three-copper piece of my money? So there's nothing for it but to lay my hands on him, even if I have to wait outside his house for hours and days. That shouldn't bother me, I'd not be wasting my time. The thing is to be sure I lay my hands on him, and I'll give him something he'll remember to the day of his death. But does he ever leave his house? Does he dare show his face out in the street? He may have enough food in the house to keep him going for weeks. Shall I ever see him except behind the bars of that window? Accursed coward, in this world and the next. I wish I could see him in hell, yelling for a glass of water. But while he's in this world is he to go on prospering, enjoying my ducats, holding them in his hands and tossing them up and catching them and hearing them clink? If he came out of the house now, at this moment, if I just happened to catch him as a result, oh, the mere thought of it is delightful. Come out, you rogue! The plague on you! The plague? That's far too mild a punishment for him. Doesn't he deserve a worse death than that?

He took a deep breath and wiped the sweat from his brow.

Fool that I am to let myself get so angry, he scolded himself. Isn't that just what the mangy jackal wants? Didn't I hear him say so, didn't I hear him laughing like a jackal? What good does cursing him do me, where does it get me? Will a hundred ducats' worth of cursing and swearing or wishing him the plague get me a penny of my money back? And if I thrash him till my arms ache, he'll still have my money. And if I don't restrain myself and do lay my hands on the contemptible scoundrel, I may get into trouble because of him. The Lord have mercy upon me, what am I doing waiting here? Did I come here to listen to his shameless and godless speeches? No, I came to see whether she – whether Niccola – O Lord – to see whether she comes out of the house by this door. O just and almighty God, help me, can it be your will that Niccola . . .?

He stopped, and for Niccola's sake did not go on invoking the just and almighty God. An idea had struck him that took possession of him and completely changed the situation. He saw a way that might lead him to his rights – that is, to his seventeen ducats.

It would work, he said to himself; perhaps it would not be too difficult; Boccetta would be the one to be cheated and he could weep for the seventeen ducats. It must be possible. True, it would put an end to my love affair. I must stop thinking about her, I must put her out of my mind. But can I? Alas, I'm only too much in love with her; it's shameful that I should still be in love with Boccetta's daughter. But supposing she isn't his daughter? I don't know yet whether she'll come out of the house. If I'm waiting for her to no purpose, that changes everything. But how shall I get my seventeen ducats back then? If she does come out through that door, though, I shall have to turn my heart to stone. But can I? Don't I still love her? And has my love for her from the outset not been greater and more ardent than hers for me? Has she not gained greater power over me than I have over her? How could that have happened to me? Where's my pride? And what has my honour to say about it?

The idea that had terrified him and caused him such agony while wandering aimlessly in the streets of Milan all night had been that she might be Boccetta's daughter. Now the strange idea struck him that if he was to carry out his plan, if it was to succeed, that would have to be true. Oh, if only it wasn't, he said to himself once more, and for the last time. No, let it be true, he contradicted himself, for the success of his plan required him to want what had previously filled him with desperation and dismay. So be it, he decided. She's Boccetta's daughter, I know it. That was the thought he hammered into his heart.

He stood staring at the door with his hands pressed to his temples, and waited. He did not know whether he felt fear or hope. He scolded and abused himself, he scorned and derided his love, he argued and quarrelled with it, and was angry at finding that it was not yet dead.

Then the door opened and he saw Niccola. He knew it was she before he saw her with her proud, ethereal walk that made her recognizable from a distance; she glided through the garden and turned into the street; she went her way like a girl in a dream.

Joachim Behaim followed behind her, and his love died, murdered by his will, betrayed by his pride. His love obstructed his plan. It could not be allowed to live.

He followed her and kept her in sight, and as he walked he prepared his plan, to be carried out the same day. After passing through the Vercelli gate he saw her hesitate for a moment and then take the road that led to the church of Sant' Eusorgio. He recalled that it was her habit to go there every day and kneel before a woodcarving of Christ in a niche in the transept and confide her hopes to Him in a few hurriedly whispered words. Once or twice when she had arrived at his room a little late she had explained that she had been with her Lord Jesus Christ at Sant' Eusorgio's and had had more to tell Him than on other days.

Go and talk to Him, then, Behaim muttered when he saw her disappearing into the dim light of the transept. God will not permit Him to listen to you. God is on my side, He showed me the way when I appealed to Him, He will help me to my rights.

With this he hurried home to wait for Niccola in his room.

She found him so busy packing his bags when she arrived that he seemed not to notice her arrival. One part of his clothes and underwear, his belt, shoes, shirts and coloured handkerchief was neatly laid out, while the other part still lay scattered about on the table, the chairs and the bed.

She was startled. For a moment she could not decide whether this boded good or evil, whether it was a beginning or an end, whether it meant goodbye for ever or being permanently together.

"Are you going?" she exclaimed anxiously. "Are you leaving Milan?"

"You said you'd follow me wherever I went," he answered without raising his eyes. "We're going by way of Lecco and across the Adda. From there it's not more than an hour into Venetian territory if good horses are available."

"Venetian territory," she murmured, for to her, who had never been farther than the neighbouring villages, that seemed a great and hazardous adventure. She snuggled up to him.

"Did you ever doubt that I'd come with you, darling?" she said. "Haven't I given you everything, my life and my soul? You only have to tell me the day and hour, and I'll be ready. Will it be today? And is it true that in Venice you can't hear yourself speak because they make such a din pounding the pepper in the vaults? And tell me, will there be room in your baggage for the things I want to take? Because I'm not completely poverty-stricken, darling – I have six pewter plates, two big ones and four small ones, as well as a salad bowl and two candlesticks, silver all of them and with the Lucardesi arms on them. I also have a copper water-jug, but it's heavy and difficult to handle, and perhaps it's not worth taking on such a long journey."

"Those things won't be very helpful to me," said Behaim, raising his head and letting the girl see the gloom and anxiety in his face. "You ask me the day and the hour, and I can't tell you. My business affairs call me to Venice, but difficulties have arisen, things haven't gone as I hoped. In short, I'm worried." Like somebody at his wits' end, he raised his arms and dropped them again.

Niccola looked at him in consternation and dismay.

"If you have worries, darling, let me share them with you," she said. "Frankly, I don't know whether I can help, but I do know there's nothing on earth I wouldn't do for you."

He laughed briefly.

"How could you possibly help me, my dear?" he said. "But if you really want to know, my business affairs are not in a very happy state. I'm short of money, I need a considerable sum, heaven knows I've never been as short as I am at this moment, and I don't know which way to turn. You can imagine that a journey like this . . ."

Niccola was shocked.

"Believe me, darling, I don't need much," she said. "If I have bread and an egg, or perhaps some fruit . . ."

Behaim dismissed this with a shrug of the shoulders.

"It isn't a matter of what we eat and drink," he explained. "A journey like this involves other, very considerable expenses. And when I've paid what I owe the landlord here I don't know whether we'll have enough left to get to Lecco and pay for a night's lodging there."

As if he were annoyed with himself for having told her all this, he went on: "So now you know how things stand. Does that help?"

Niccola sighed, and thought hard for a moment. Then she said anxiously: "Is it a lot of money you're short of? Is it a large sum?"

"Forty ducats," he answered. "It's easy to say that, it sounds as if it's hardly worth mentioning, but it's incredible how much it is when you need it and don't know where to get it from." And he drew his hand across his brow like a man oppressed with cares.

"Forty ducats," Niccola said, and for a while she said

nothing. She was thinking about her father's money, which he loved more than his own eyes and kept carefully hidden from her. Nevertheless she had not failed to notice in what holes and corners, behind which stone blocks, under which floor tiles it was hidden. She read care and worry in her lover's face, but did not find it easy to make up her mind.

"Forty ducats," she repeated. "Forty ducats. Perhaps it might be possible, darling. I might be able to get them for you."

"You?" Behaim exclaimed with pleasure and excitement in his voice. "Are you being serious? Really? Could you? That would clear it all up. But it can't be true, I can't believe it. You're not being serious."

In thought she was back in her father's house. It's not wrong what I'm going to do, she said to herself. It's all right to take what I'm entitled to. I'm leaving him, but he wouldn't give me even the tiniest trousseau. He wouldn't even give me travelling expenses. Forty ducats! He'll notice it quickly enough, of course. He remembers every log of wood he has in the house.

The thought did not frighten her. In her imagination she was already on the way to Venice.

"I'm perfectly serious," she said. "Don't you believe me, darling? You've no idea what I'm capable of doing for you."

"If you're really being serious, if you can really get the money, don't waste time," Behaim said to her. "Don't keep me waiting long. Hurry."

Chapter 12

Ludovico il Moro, the Duke of Milan, lay on his sick-bed in a room in the ducal castle known as the Hall of the Shepherds and Fauns – the latter were represented on two Flemish carpets that adorned the walls. He was troubled by pains in the midriff, and a swelling in his knee-joint caused him acute pain, but the attentions of the physician on whom he relied, who had been summoned in haste, had so far given him little relief. Antonio Benincasa, a gentleman-in-waiting, was that day enjoying the privilege of reading Dante to the sick duke. He stood at the foot of the bed with a copy of the *Purgatorio* open in his hands, and in his resonant voice he had just finished reading the eleventh canto, in which Oderisi da Gubbio, the book illuminator, laments the transience of earthly fame. Tommaso Lancia, the head of the duke's secret chancery, was in a recess, immersed in his papers; he had come to report to the duke everything that had happened in the past few days in the city of Milan. He employed several dozen persons of high and low degree whose task it was to provide him with daily reports on everything, both good and ill, that was going on in the city: what was being planned, what was actually being done, what news and rumours were in circulation, who had arrived and who had left, as well as anything else that was worthy of note. For it was necessary to counter the efforts of the French court, which was doing everything it could to diminish the duke's reputation, power and wealth, and to that end was lavish with money and promises of all sorts.

It was known, moreover, that there were many persons of rank and reputation who in given circumstances would not hesitate to tear down the city gates and replace them with triumphal arches to the greater glory of the King of France on his entry into Milan.

Master Zabatto, the physician, was standing by his copper tripod and heating over a heap of glowing coal the mixture he was proposing to give the duke. The page-boy Giamino was ready to give the patient wine at his request, or to smooth his pillow or make him fresh cold compresses, or to carry out whatever orders the duke or the physician might impart.

Outside in the corridors and galleries gentlemen-in-waiting, state councillors, dignitaries, members of the household, chancery secretaries and officers of the castle guard stood ready to be summoned to the sick-room to perform some service for the duke if called upon, or to give information, or to discuss whatever it might be – urgent business or some obscure passage in the *Purgatorio*. At brief intervals the notes of a lyre could be heard: the Fennel, one of the court musicians in attendance with the others, was passing the time by playing disconnected tunes, alternately suggesting a question and an answer and effectively conducting a conversation with himself.

On the main staircase Messer Leonardo, who had been to the treasurer's office to collect some money due to him, met Matteo Bossi, the gentleman-in-waiting responsible for the ducal table. When Bossi told him that the sick duke had put himself in the hands of Master Zabatto, Leonardo expressed in no uncertain terms his displeasure at the choice of such a physician, whose knowledge and ability he held as of no account. The gentleman-in-waiting coughed as he listened to him, for he had respiratory trouble and had continually to clear his throat to get a little air.

"To think that a man like that should have the impudence to call himself a doctor and an anatomist," said Leonardo indignantly. "Knowledge. What knowledge does he possess? Can be explain to me why sleepiness and boredom both induce the strange activity known as yawning? Can he tell me how it is that sorrow, suffering and physical pain seek a little relief by producing drops of a salty liquid from our eyes? Or why fear and cold both cause the human frame to tremble? Ask him; he won't know what to answer. He can't tell you the number of muscles needed to maintain the mobility of the tongue, enabling it to speak and praise its Maker, and he doesn't know the place and the importance of the spleen and the liver in the human system. Can he explain to me the nature of that wonderful instrument, the heart, devised and made by the Supreme Designer? He cannot. He's nothing but a pharmacist who can also bleed people. Maybe he can set a dislocated leg. But to be a physician he should try to understand what a human being is and what life is."

The gentleman-in-waiting agreed with the indignant Leonardo by telling him of his own experiences.

"I must say I agree with you, Messer Leonardo, he couldn't do anything for me either," he said, "though the fact of the matter is that the other doctors whom I consulted did no better. Well, I'm still alive, and I can still perform my duties. But if my trouble gets worse? What then? What will happen to the ducal table? Who will take over the responsibility? Woe is me, I can't bear to think of it. Believe me, only when it's too late will His Highness realize what a servant he had in me." He sighed, pressed and shook Leonardo's hand, and went down the stairs coughing and clearing his throat.

Up in the gallery a group of courtiers in attendance were passing the time in discussion; after disposing of a number of questions they were now on the old problem of which earthly possessions entitled their owner to call himself a happy man. The first to answer the question was the secretary Ferriero, who was responsible for drafting the ducal dispatches, a task that kept him so busy that he generally had no time to clean the ink off his fingers.

"Happiness," he said, straightening the pile of papers he was holding, "would be having hounds, falcons, a hunt, and a fine stud."

"I'm not so ambitious," said a young officer of the castle guard. "I'd consider myself happy if I won a brace of gold pieces at knucklebones this evening."

Tiraboschi, the state councillor who owned two profitable vineyards and was known as a great economizer, said: "If I could invite a few friends to dine with me every day and talk intelligently about the arts and the sciences and the art of government, that's what I should regard as great good fortune. But," he sighed, "a rich table and highly trained servants to wait on us would be necessary; and unfortunately my means do not extend to that."

"What is happiness but having the poison of life wrapped in a golden shawl?" said Lascaris, the Greek who had been made homeless by the fall of Constantinople and was now responsible for the education of the duke's two sons.

"There's only one thing that I regard as really precious and irreplaceable, and that is time. He who can do whatever he likes with it is happy and rich. I, gentlemen, am one of the poorest of the poor."

This complaint by the state councillor della Teglia nevertheless expressed self-satisfaction and pride rather than regret, for the duke had the greatest confidence in him and for years had been entrusting him with political missions to the Italian courts, great and small; no sooner had he completed one of these missions than the next awaited him.

"Happiness, real happiness, is making things that do not perish with the day but survive for centuries," the ducal confectioner said with resignation.

"In that case the only place in which to look for happiness would be the street of the boilermakers," said the young Guarniero, one of the duke's pages, who had the highest regard for the court confectioner's transient creations.

"Happiness is being able to be what one wanted to be in one's youth," said Cencio, the horse-trainer who was responsible for the reins, harness and saddles of all the horses in the ducal stables. "All other gifts of fortune I regard as chaff," he went on, "and so I might well regard myself as a happy man if only I heard an occasional word of appreciation of what I do. But, as everyone knows . . ."

He fell silent, shrugged his shoulders, and left it to others to decide whether he could be described as happy in those circumstances.

"As my friends know," said the poet Bellincioli, "in the course of many years I have succeeded in putting together a collection of rare and important books, as well as a number of paintings by the best masters. The possession of these treasures has not made me a happy man, but merely given me the satisfaction of being able to tell myself that I haven't totally wasted my life. And I have to content myself with that, for in this world happiness is not granted to thinking minds."

He saw Leonardo approaching, nodded a greeting to him and went on, hoping to be overheard by him. "Another thing that bothers me is that there is a gap in my library that has been vacant for years. It is reserved for Messer Leonardo's treatise on painting which that great master began a considerable time ago. But who can say when it will be finished?"

Leonardo, who was absorbed in thought, neither noticed Bellincioli's greeting nor heard what he said.

"He hasn't noticed that we're talking about him. He's not in this small world, but up among the stars. Perhaps he's working out how the moon manages to stay in equilibrium."

"He looks gloomy," Becchi, the gentleman in charge of the ducal household pointed out, "as if he were musing on how to paint the destruction of Sodom, or the despair of those unable to escape the Flood."

"They say he's dreamed up amazing inventions which would bring a quick victory to hard-pressed garrisons and also to those besieging them," remarked the young officer of the castle guard.

"He's certainly deep in thought," said the Greek Lascaris. "Perhaps he's trying to work out how to weigh in carats the spirit of God in which the whole universe is contained."

"Or whether there's anyone else like him in the world," said the state councillor Tiraboschi with a sneer.

"We know you don't like him," said Bellincioli. "You don't know him, but everyone who does know him even slightly adores him."

Tiraboschi twisted his narrow lips into a superior smile, and the talk turned to other things.

Messer Leonardo had had neither eyes nor ears for this courtly gathering, and his thoughts as he walked through the gallery were indeed high in the sky; he was thinking about birds that are able to soar without beating their wings and depend on the wind alone; this mystery had long filled him with awe and amazement. But the lady Lucrezia Crivelli brought him down to earth with a tap on the shoulder.

"Messer Leonardo, I could have wished for nothing better than to meet you," the duke's mistress said to him, "and if you will be kind enough to listen to me . . ."

"Madam, I am completely at your disposal," Leonardo replied, dismissing from his mind the herons soaring in the clouds.

"I am told, and indeed every one assures me, that you are devoting yourself to architecture, anatomy, and even military science instead of applying yourself, as is His Highness's wish . . ."

Leonardo interrupted her.

"That is true," he said. "I could satisfy His Highness better than anyone else, with all the things that you have mentioned. And if His Highness graciously consented to receive me, I would reveal to him some secrets concerning the construction of military machines. I could show him drawings of unassailable chariots I have devised which could be driven into the enemy's ranks spreading death and destruction, and not even the largest body of armed men would be able to resist them."

"Please don't talk to me about those chariots," Lucrezia exclaimed. "Is it ideas of battle and bloodshed that have kept you so long from the peaceful art of painting?"

"I would also remind His Highness," Leonardo went on eagerly, "that the Adda must be given a new course so that it may carry ships, drive mills, oil presses and other things, and irrigate meadows and gardens. I have worked out where pools and dams, locks and weirs, will have to be constructed to regulate the flow of water. All this will improve the land and provide His Highness with sixty thousand ducats of annual revenue. You raise your brows, madam, you shake your head? Do you think the amount I have mentioned is exaggerated? Do you think an error has crept into my calculations?"

"You speak of many things, Messer Leonardo," Lucrezia said, "but you have avoided mentioning the thing that is closest to His Highness's heart and mine. I mean the picture you have been asked to finish. The picture of the Saviour and His disciples. I'm told you look askance at your brushes nowadays and pick them up only with reluctance and displeasure. And it is about that and not about oil presses and war chariots that I should like to hear you speak."

Messer Leonardo saw that he had not succeeded in avoiding the questions about the *Last Supper*, and this vexed him. But he did not lose his innate equanimity.

"Let me assure you, madam, that my attention is completely concentrated on that painting," he said, "and what people with little understanding of these matters have told you is as remote from the truth as darkness is from light. And I have appealed to the reverend father with all the sincerity with which one appeals to Christ to have patience and at last to stop complaining to me every day and pestering me and putting pressure on me."

"I thought it would give you pleasure to finish such a pious work. Or do you so feel so worn out and exhausted by working on it that . . ."

"Madam," Leonardo interrupted, "I am so gripped by this picture that it cannot possibly tire me, for that is my nature."

"Then why do you not treat that old man like a good son treats his father by falling in with his wishes, which are also His Highness's?" asked the duke's mistress.

"The work awaits its hour," replied Leonardo. "It will be finished to the honour of God and the fame of this city. No one will persuade me to let it redound to my dishonour."

"So is it true, as many say," Lucrezia asked, "that you are afraid of making mistakes and thus attracting adverse criticism? Is it true that you, whom they call the greatest master of the age, suffer in your work from imagining you see mistakes where others see marvels?"

"What you reproach me with, madam, whether you do so with a greater measure of kindness or of charm, is truly not the case," Leonardo replied, "though I should very much like to be what you say I am, to some extent at any rate. The truth is, however, that I am as attached to this work as the lover is to his beloved. And, as you know, the beloved is sometimes ill humoured and coy and rejects her passionate wooer."

"Such pleasantries are beside the point," said the duke's mistress, who saw herself in any reference to love. "You know, Messer Leonardo, how devoted I am to you. But it is possible that the obstinacy with which you refrain from working on this picture might arouse His Highness's displeasure, in which case you would not remain for long in His Highness's grace and favour."

When Messer Leonardo heard these words he imagined himself pursuing the arts and sciences in some strange and distant land, without friends or companions, homeless, lonely and in great want.

"Perhaps it will be my fate henceforth to live in poverty," he said. "But I have to thank nature's generous abundance for the fact that wherever I go I find new things to learn; and that, madam, is the task allotted me by the Mover of All Things. And even though henceforth I shall spend my life in another country among men who speak a different tongue, I shall not cease to think of the fame and best advantage of this duchy, and may God keep it under His protection."

With these words he bent over Lucrezia's hand as if he were saying goodbye for ever.

At that moment the page Giamino approached her with a deep bow and told her that the duke desired her presence, for the head of the secret chancery had finished his report. Leonardo turned to go, but Giamino stopped him with a shy gesture.

"Forgive me, sir," he said, "but I have some news for you too, and it is not easy to impart, for it is not the kind of news that one is glad to hear. But you will certainly not wish me to withhold from you something that may perhaps be of importance."

"So you have to tell me that I have fallen into disfavour with His Highness, and that he has used angry and bitter words about me?"

The boy shook his head vigorously.

"Not so, messere," he said, "the duke has never talked about you like that, believe me. He mentions your name only with the greatest possible respect. What I have to tell you is not about you, but about one of your friends. Messer Lancia calls him Mancino and says he has often been seen in your company, and what his Christian name is I don't know."

"No one knows it," said Leonardo. "And what has happened to him?"

"He was found fatally wounded this morning in the garden of the house by the well, lying in a pool of blood," Giamino said. "Messer Lancia says it looks as if his brow was smashed in with an axe. And, sir, I have to tell you that the house where it happened is Boccetta's – the Boccetta you know about – and the duke has ordered an investigation. Perhaps this time . . ."

"And where is Mancino now?" Leonardo asked.

"Forgive me for not having told you at once," Giamino said. "Messer Lancia says he was taken to the silk weavers' hospital, where he's awaiting a priest and the viaticum."

Messer Leonardo found Mancino in a room under the rafters on the third floor of the hospital. There were no beds here, nothing but straw over which coarse striped sheets were spread. Mancino lay with his eyes shut, his lined cheeks were flushed with fever, his hands were in continual restless motion, he had flung off the blanket, and his head and brow were swathed in bandages. Two of his friends, d'Oggiono the painter and the organist Martegli, were standing over him, and the organist, who kept his head bent to avoid hitting the rafters, was holding a jug of wine.

"He's not asleep; he has just asked for something to drink," d'Oggiono said, "but he's only allowed wine mixed half and half with water, and he doesn't like that very much."

"He's in a bad way," the organist whispered, bending still lower to talk into Leonardo's ear. "A priest has been here and heard his confession and given him the last rites. The surgeon said that it might perhaps have been possible to do something for him if help had arrived more quickly, but the people who found him appealed to all the saints and brought consecrated objects from the church, but no one thought of sending for a surgeon. Not till he was brought here was the wound cleaned and the bleeding stopped. It looks as if he clashed with Boccetta, for he was found close to his house."

"Something to drink," Mancino said softly. He opened his eyes, and sipped from the jug the organist held to his lips. Then he caught sight of Leonardo, a smile flitted across his face, and he raised his hand in greeting.

"Welcome, Leonardo," he said. "It's a great pleasure and honour to see you here, though you'd do better to turn your attention to matters of greater importance than my present state. Just as I was about to leave and was going to jump out of the window he tried his axe on me – he behaved more like a fool than a rogue – and the idiot gave me a bloody gash on the forehead. It's no more than that, it's something nobody dies of, but I thought it a good idea to put myself in a surgeon's care for a few hours."

Again he asked for something to drink, took a draught, and made a grimace. Then he pointed to the man lying on the straw beside him and went on: "He's in a sorry state. His mule threw him, and kicked him so severely that no one could lift him to his feet again, the surgeon said. I was luckier."

The fever took hold of him and he became confused. "You three up there, Father, Son and Holy Ghost," he said, "don't squabble about my soul, but leave it where it is, and you, Blessed Trinity, be patient, I shan't run away, I've always been a good Christian, I was never one of those who go to church to steal the candles. The devil take you, landlord, for not giving me any wine other than this, you've dipped it three times in holy water in your cellar and made it unfit for a Christian to drink."

He lay for a time with his eyes closed, breathing loudly. Then, when his breathing grew quieter, he opened his eyes.

The fever had left him, and he made it clear that he knew the state he was in.

"*Je m'en vais en pays loingtain*," he said, and shook his friends' hands and bade them farewell. "Join me in lamenting my wasted days, which passed as swiftly as a weaver's shuttle. If only it had been granted to me to die fighting the Turks or pagans for the victory of the Christian faith, God would gladly have forgiven my sinful life, and all the saints and angels in paradise would have come dancing towards me and welcomed my soul with psalms and the notes of the viola. But as it is I shall appear before God's judgment seat just as I am and have been all my life, a drinker, gambler, loafer, brawler, whoremonger . . ."

"The Disposer of our Destinies knows that you are none of those things, but a poet," said Leonardo, grasping Mancino's hand. "But tell me, what on earth made you pick a quarrel with Boccetta?"

"Nothing happens without a cause. Find it, and you will understand what has happened – aren't those your own words, my Leonardo? I have often heard you say them. Is the world not full of bitterness and perfidy? A woman came to me and wept and was at her wits' end in her grief, and if anyone could die of shame and sorrow, she would have preceded me. So I took the money from her and I climbed through the window to give it back to Boccetta, and I did so like a real fool, making so much noise that he started out of his sleep and must have thought I had come to rob him. And if you're still in need of Judas's face, my Leonardo, I know the man who has it. Look for your Judas no longer, for I have found him. Except that he did not pocket thirty pieces of silver, but seventeen ducats."

He closed his eyes and struggled for breath.

"If I have understood him rightly," said d'Oggiono, "he's talking about the German who claimed seventeen ducats from

Boccetta. He bet me a ducat that by hook or by crook he would get his money back, for he was not a person to be cheated out of seventeen ducats. And today he let me know that he had won the bet in the most glorious fashion, and that Boccetta's seventeen ducats were in his pocket, and that he was coming early tomorrow morning to collect his winnings. And so I've still got to go to three or four houses today where they owe me money and try to raise a ducat, for I have only two carlini in my purse."

"I should like to see this German whom Mancino calls a Judas," said Leonardo, "and I should like him to tell us how he got his money from Boccetta."

"Something to drink," Mancino moaned.

"You can ask Boccetta himself," said the organist, holding the wine jug to Mancino's lips with one hand and pointing to the door with the other.

"There he is, by the holy cross," d'Oggiono exclaimed.

Two city pikemen had entered the room, bringing with them Boccetta as a prisoner. He stood between them in his shabby coat and worn shoes and with his hands tied behind his back, but he behaved as arrogantly as if he were a great lord escorted by two of his servants.

"There you are, sir," one of the escorts said. "We've done what you want, so now hurry up and say your piece, but keep it brief, because we have no time to waste."

Boccetta recognized Messer Leonardo and greeted him as one nobleman greeting another. Then he noticed Mancino and, with the two pikemen close behind him, went to where he was lying.

"Do you recognize me?" he said. "I came here for the good of your immortal soul, I came here in a spirit of Christian charity to lead you back to the way of honesty. But take note that when you made off you scattered the stolen ducats on the floor as if they were beans or lentils. I had to crawl all over the place to pick them up. But seventeen ducats are still missing. I couldn't find them though I hunted for them everywhere, and they don't belong to me, but to a pious servant of the

Church, a venerable priest who gave them to me to look after, so they are holy, consecrated money. Tell me where you've buried or hidden them, I ask you that for the salvation of your soul."

Mancino asked d'Oggiono for the blanket, for he was having a shivering fit. When the blanket was over him he answered Boccetta.

"Just keep looking then," he said. "Creep and crawl and slave and sweat until you've found them. For you know that he who has the money has the honour."

"So you won't tell me?" Boccetta shouted, pale with fury and struggling vainly to free his hands. "Then go to hell, and may a thousand devils take their pleasure with you, I wish I could . . ."

"Take this pest out of here," d'Oggiono said to the two pikemen. "Why did you bring the scoundrel here, he belongs to the hangman."

"All the way here he implored us to take him to see this poor devil so that he might beg his forgiveness," one of them said.

"What did you call me, young gentleman?" Boccetta said, turning to d'Oggiono. "A scoundrel? And I belong to the hangman, you said? Well, it's all the same to me, abuse doesn't affect me. But when I'm free again and master of my own actions it will cost you a great deal of money, young gentleman, for you'll have to pay me damages. You have heard what he said, Leonardo, and you will be my witness."

"As the court that he daily mocks and derides has at last laid its hands on him, take him away," said Leonardo.

"*Nostre Seigneur se taist tout quoy*," Mancino whispered, and those were his last words in this world. He answered no more questions. All that was to be heard was his quiet moaning, which later gave way to a death rattle, which went on until the early evening hour when he died.

Chapter 13

While they waited for Joachim Behaim to appear in d'Oggiono's room Leonardo looked at the wooden chest decorated with pictures of the *Wedding Feast at Cana*, and he was pleased with the work that the young painter had finished the day before.

"I see that in this thankless and tiresome task you have borne in mind what is the rudder, what is the rein of all painting, that is to say, perspective," he said. "The drawing is good, too, and so is the way you have applied your paint. You have painted the figures so that one can easily tell from their posture what is uppermost in their mind. That mercenary came to the wedding only for the drink and to drink as much as possible; and it's obvious to anyone that the bride's father is an honest man who will never say anything dishonourable and will keep his promises to the bridegroom. And look at the steward of the feast – it's clear how concerned he is that all the guests should enjoy themselves."

"And what about Christ?" asked d'Oggiono, who could not get enough praise.

"You have given His features nobility, and the Madonna is very sweet and charming. The only thing is the road up the hill: look at the poplars, they don't cast a shadow. If you feel uncertain about painting landscape, simply look at nature and real life."

"Oh, dear," d'Oggiono exclaimed. "Yes, I know, and I'm ashamed that this dreadful *Wedding Feast* is such a failure. I've bungled the job. If the man wasn't coming to fetch it tomorrow, I'd just as soon smash the chest to pieces and use it for kindling."

"It's a great success, a masterly piece of work," Leonardo said to console him. "I've nothing but praise for the way you've handled your light and shade."

Meanwhile Simoni the woodcarver was telling his friend the organist Martegli for the third time of the astonishing adventure he had had the day before.

"I crossed the road from my workshop to the church of Sant' Eusorgio, as I do several times a day, and she was kneeling in despair in front of that Christ – a pitiful piece of work it is, the boy who holds my chisel could make a better job. God knows how long she had been there, sobbing her heart out, her face distraught, tears running down her cheeks; and when I saw her like that, I don't know how, but at last I plucked up courage to talk to her. You won't believe it, but I took her home with me. I told her my father was an old man, ill and bed-ridden, and it would be a Christian act if she took over the task of looking after him at night; and she looked at me, I don't know whether she recognized me or not, I have often greeted her in the street, in short, believe it or not, she came with me. I think she was beyond caring what happened to her. During the night I heard her weeping, but this morning, when I took some bread and milk to her and to my father, she had a smile for me. Perhaps, after all she's been through, and when time has passed and she has got used to me . . . Tommaso, if she stayed with me, if I could hold on to her, I'd think myself the happiest man in Christendom. Yes, look at me, I don't look like a lover with my stubby legs, my paunch and bald head, and calluses on my hands from working with gouge and chisel. Perhaps my head is full of idle hopes and plans, and perhaps you're right, Tommaso, when you say I'm like those who try to turn copper into gold. For she still thinks of nothing but him."

"I remember him," the organist said, "and I can understand that she fell in love with him. He's young and tall and handsome."

The door opened, and the man they were talking about, Joachim Behaim, came in and greeted the company. He was in travelling clothes and riding boots, and looked all ready to mount his horse and leave the city.

He saw Leonardo, and at once went up to him and paid him his respects.

"I have long wanted to make your acquaintance and enjoy your company," he said respectfully. "It's some time since I first saw you; it was in the old courtyard at the duke's castle, on the day I sold His Most Serene Highness a Barbary and a Neapolitan. Perhaps you remember, sir."

"Yes, I remember the occasion well," said Leonardo, though it was only the Barbary horse that he had in mind.

"And since then," Behaim went on, "I have often heard your name mentioned, always in the most flattering terms, and have heard things about you that are quite exceptional."

He bowed once more, and then greeted d'Oggiono and the other two.

"I too," said Leonardo, "have very much wanted to meet you, particularly as I have a favour to ask you."

"Should I have the good fortune to be able to help you in any way, you only have to ask me," Behaim said very politely.

"That is very kind of you," said Leonardo. "What I should like you to do is to tell us how you contrived to recover your money, your seventeen ducats, from Boccetta, who is, after all, well known throughout Milan as a scoundrel and a thief."

"And thanks to that I've shamefully lost my bet and have now to pay up, hard though it is to do so," said d'Oggiono.

"Water from the spring is always better than water from the jug," said the woodcarver. "It's always better to go to the source."

"It's not much of a story, hardly worth telling," Behaim said, taking a chair and sitting down like the others. "On the very first day I told Boccetta that I was not a person who could be cheated of his money and that anyone who tried to take me on had always lived to regret it, because he always came off second best."

"We are very anxious to hear your story," said Leonardo.

"Well, then, to put it in a nutshell, let me begin by telling you that here in Milan I met a girl whom I liked more than any I had ever met. I don't want to boast, but I have been accustomed, and it has been granted me, to get from women what I want from them without great difficulty, and so it was on this occasion. Gentlemen, I believed I had found in her the woman I had sought for all my life. She was tall and slender, beautiful and charming. Her proud and attractive walk made her recognizable from a thousand paces, and she was dutiful and modest with it; she disliked ostentation, was devoted to me and had no eyes for others."

He stopped, stared ahead of him deep in thought, and then drew his hand vigorously across his brow as if he were trying to drive away the vision he had conjured up by what he had been saying. Then he went on:

"She was the woman I had always sought for, and here in Milan I found her. But one evening only a few days ago I went to the Lamb to drink some wine and talk to one of the regular customers there; and there I was told" – he pointed to d'Oggiono and the woodcarver – "that the woman I loved was Boccetta's daughter."

He leapt to his feet and walked up and down in great agitation. Then he resumed his seat and went on: "To think that of all the thousands of men in Milan Boccetta should be her father. But that was what happened to me. You see, gentlemen, how badly fate can treat an honourable man."

"Did Judas Iscariot also call himself an honourable man?" the woodcarver whispered to the organist.

"I cannot describe to you, gentlemen, the thoughts that assailed me," Behaim went on. "I'm ashamed to say I still loved her even then, and I was filled with utter dismay when I realized it. My suffering was almost beyond endurance, I could neither eat nor sleep. But eventually I decided to master it and allow it no more room inside me."

"And you managed that so easily?' the woodcarver asked.

Behaim was silent for a moment.

"No, it was not easy," he replied. "It needed a great effort to master the spell she still exercised over me. But I came to my senses, I made it clear to myself that I must not live with her. For that meant not merely sleeping with her and, as the saying goes, dropping my hook, but sharing food and drink and going to church with her, sleeping and waking, and sharing my cares and pleasures with her – with her, Boccetta's daughter. Even if she were the very gates of paradise she could not be my wife, she could not go on being my mistress. I loved her only too much, and my pride and honour would not allow that."

"Yes," said Leonardo, thinking of someone else. "His pride and honour did not allow that."

"Who it was who helped me in the matter, who put me right, whether it was my guardian angel or God Himself or Our Lady – I don't know. But when I had got over my love, everything was simple."

He fell silent for a moment, and then he went on: "She came to me, as she did every day, and she had love-making in mind, but I acted as if I had serious worries. I told her I was short of money, I urgently needed forty ducats and didn't know where to get them from – I was in serious trouble. She was rather startled, and thought about it for a while, and then she told me not to worry, she knew a way of getting the money, and I took her word for it. Don't misunderstand me, gentlemen, I didn't need the money, I have silk and woollen cloth to the value of eight hundred sequins in the warehouses at Venice which I can turn profitably into cash at any time."

"I thought you made your living as a horse-dealer," Leonardo interrupted.

"One can make money dealing in anything," Behaim explained; "today horses, tomorrow horseshoe nails, or groats as well as pearls or spices from India. I deal in anything that brings in money, salves, skin creams, rouge from the Levant, or another day in carpets from Alexandria – if you happen to know where flax can be bought cheaply, tell me, for a bad flax harvest is expected this year."

"He deals in everything, did you hear?" the woodcarver

whispered to the organist. "He'd deal in the blood of Christ if he had it."

"But to come back to what you want to hear about," Behaim went on. "Next day she came back with the money, and she counted it out to me, forty ducats. She thought she had done me a great service, and was in high spirits. I shan't tell you in detail what happened next, gentlemen, what I told her and what she said, because it would bore you. To put it in a nutshell, she admitted she had stolen the money from her father, she did it at night when he was asleep, and I told her it was wrong and dishonest and I disapproved of it most strongly, it offended against Christianity and the child's duty to love its parents and that, as she had now shown me her true nature, she could be mine no longer, she must go, and I didn't want to see her again. At first she thought I was joking. She laughed and said: 'That's a fine thing from a man who says he loves me,' but then, when she realized I was being serious, she begged and entreated and wept and behaved as if she were in despair, but I had made up my mind not to listen to her and took no notice of her lamentations. I deducted from the money the seventeen ducats that were due to me and gave her a receipt, as was right and proper, and gave her back the rest of the money, and so everything was done legally. For I only want to have and to hold what is my own, and I'm not concerned with what belongs to others. And then I offered her my hand in farewell and told her to go and not come back; and she grew angry and had the audacity to call me a wicked man. But I remembered the words that you" – he turned to d'Oggiono and pointed to the picture of the *Wedding Feast at Cana* on the chest – "put into the Saviour's mouth at that marriage: 'Woman, what have I to do with thee?' And I showed her the door."

"So you threw away a great love like a cheap ring bought at a flea market," the organist exclaimed indignantly.

"Sir, I don't know who you are or what you mean," Behaim snapped at him. "Are you criticizing me for giving back his money and his daughter to a desperate father?"

"Certainly not, no one's criticizing you," Leonardo said

appeasingly. "You pleaded your cause against Boccetta very well . . ."

"It was a just cause," said Behaim.

"Certainly, it was a just cause," said Leonardo, "and therefore I shall show you the honour to which you are entitled by ensuring that you shall be remembered in Milan. For the face of a man like you is worth drawing and being handed down to those who will come after us."

He produced his sketch-book and silver pencil from under his belt.

"You are doing me an honour that I highly appreciate," Behaim assured him, and he sat upright in his chair and stroked his dark, well tended beard.

"And your love for her," the woodcarver asked him as Leonardo set about drawing his portrait, "or what you called your love, is it now completely dead?"

Behaim shrugged his shoulders.

"That's my business and not yours," he said. "But, if you want to know, I have not got her out of my mind yet; she's not a person who can be so easily forgotten. But I think I shall stop thinking about her when I've left Milan and put thirty or forty miles behind me."

"And where are you going?" d'Oggiono wanted to know.

"To Venice," Behaim replied. "I shall be staying for four or five days before sailing to Constantinople."

"I like travelling too," said the woodcarver, "but only where I can see cows grazing." He meant that he was not such a fool as to risk his life on the open sea or any other stormy water.

"Are you going to the Turks again?" d'Oggiono exclaimed. "Don't you fear for your life among people who are so fierce and ruthless in spilling Christian blood?"

"The Turks at home and in their own country are not half so black as they are painted, just as the devil at home in hell is perhaps a very good paterfamilias," said Behaim. "But you haven't forgotten that you are to pay me a ducat? You have got to pay up, if for no other reason than to teach you to treat me and my like with greater respect in future."

D'Oggiono sighed and produced a pile of silver from his pocket. Behaim took it and counted it. He thanked d'Oggiono and slipped the money into his purse.

"Hold the purse in your hand for a minute," Leonardo said, smiling and nodding at Behaim. And, while Behaim held the purse in his hand, ready to pocket it, Leonardo added a few strokes, and the drawing was finished.

Behaim rose and stretched his limbs. Then he asked Leonardo whether he might look at the sketch-book. He looked at his portrait, professed his great pleasure with it, and was lavish with his praise.

"Yes, that's me," he said, "it's really an excellent likeness. And you did it so quickly too. The things I have heard about you are certainly not exaggerated. Yes, sir, you understand your craft, and there are many who should take you as an example."

He turned a page of the sketch-book and read with surprise some of Leonardo's notes: "Christofano, who comes from Bergamo, take note of him. He has the face you have been thinking of for Philip. Talk to him about the things that worry him: plagues, the danger of war, and the growing burden of taxes. He's to be found in the Via Sant'Arcangelo, where the fine flying buttress is in the House of the Two Doves over the cutler's workshop."

"You write as the Turks do, from right to left," Behaim remarked. "And who is this Philip whose face this seems to be about?"

"Philip was one of Christ's disciples," Leonardo explained. "In my picture I want to show Christ among His disciples, and want to put Philip in the foreground as one who had a great love for the Saviour."

"Good gracious," said Behaim. "I see that to paint a picture like that you have to do a great deal more than trouble about your paints and brushes."

And he handed the sketch-book back to Leonardo, and said he was sorry not to be able to enjoy the gentlemen's company any longer, but time was pressing, his horse was already saddled. He took his coat and his cap, bowed deeply to Messer Leonardo, waved to d'Oggiono and the woodcarver and, with a brief nod to the organist Martegli to whom he had taken a dislike, he left.

"There he goes," d'Oggiono said bitterly, shaking his fists. "And to think that Mancino had to die because of a man like that."

"Die?" said Leonardo. "I think of it differently. He has proudly rejoined the whole and thus escaped from earthly imperfection."

He hid the sketch-book under his belt and spoke with undisguised pleasure and triumph. "Now I have what I need," he said. "And it will be seen in this work that heaven and earth and even God Himself have visibly lent a hand to help me by sending me this man. Now I shall show those who come after me that I too have lived on this earth."

"And now at last," said d'Oggiono, "you will satisfy the duke whom you serve and promote the reputation of this city."

"I serve no duke and no prince," said Leonardo, "and I belong to no city, no country, and no kingdom. I serve only my passion for observing, understanding, ordering and creating, and I belong to my work."

Chapter 14

Eight years later, in the autumn of 1506, Joachim Behaim, coming from the Levant, was again on his way to Milan on business. He landed in Venice, where he stayed only a few hours, for he had nothing to put in the warehouses. The goods he had for sale, contained in two silk-lined bags, were precious stones. One of the bags contained cut sapphires, emeralds and rubies, a dozen of them altogether, and all fine specimens; the other contained stones of lesser value, amethysts, yellow topazes and hyacinths; and he wanted to offer the contents of both to the French nobles and officers who were stationed in Milan, for Milan was now in the hands of the French.

For in 1501, when the King of France descended from the Alpine passes with an army of Frenchmen and Swiss and invaded Lombardy, two of Il Moro's commanders treacherously surrendered to the French. Both the Holy Roman Emperor and the King of Naples failed to fulfil their treaty obligations and neither came to his aid, and so he ended by losing his dukedom, his property, his friends and finally his freedom. He fell into the hands of Louis XII, the King of France, and spent his last years in a monastery on top of a rock in the town of Loches in Touraine on the bank of the River Indre.

The Milanese got on well with their new masters. If we have to have foreigners within our walls, they said, better the French than the Spaniards. For the Spaniards are sullen and boring people who are always going down on their knees in churches, while wherever the French go they take enjoyment and gaiety with them. And as for their Christianity, they say: Serve God?

Why not? But let us not forget that it is sometimes a good thing to wander awhile in the ways of the world.

So Joachim Behaim was on his way to Milan. But when he stopped in Verona to find a night's accommodation for himself and his horse, he was struck by the remarkable behaviour of the inhabitants, for which he could find no explanation.

People looked at him, stared at him, put their heads together and whispered. Others seemed terrified at the sight of him. They stopped, shook their heads, and made the sign of the cross once, twice or even three times, as if to avert an evil. Others quite shamelessly pointed at him, or made ill-concealed gestures to draw their companions' attention to him.

Hell and damnation, he cursed quietly to himself. What's the matter with them? What sort of behaviour is it to stare at someone like this? Haven't they ever before set eyes on a German merchant who has come from the Levant?

At the first inn the landlord stared at him and then slammed the door in his face, exclaiming "Heaven forbid," and in spite of all knocking, shouting and swearing he refused to open it again. The next landlord he tried was similarly taken aback by Behaim's appearance, but remained polite. He was very sorry, he said, but the place was over-filled already; with the best will in the world he could find no room for him, and with repeated assurances of his profound regret he showed Behaim the door.

Only at the third inn was Behaim given a room for himself and a place in the stable and a nosebag for his horse. True, the landlord looked at him in amazement and alarm and was too taken aback to speak.

"What sort of behaviour is it to stare at me like that?" Behaim snapped. "And how long are you keeping me standing and waiting here? Let me tell you that by nature I'm not exactly patient."

"I beg your pardon, sir," said the landlord, who by now had recovered his composure. "You resemble a certain person whom I saw recently. I thought you were he, for there's an amazing resemblance."

After showing Behaim to his room and telling a stable-boy to give the horse a rub-down, he turned to the waiter, who was just as startled as he was, and explained his behaviour.

"What is one to do?" he said. "What is one to say? It's well known that evil, even the greatest evil, is willed and put into the world by God."

At this inn Behaim struck up an acquaintance with a Tyrolese merchant prince who had come from Bologna and was on his way back to Innsbruck. Behaim found out at dinner that this Tyrolese merchant had not been struck by the townspeople's remarkable and in some instances shameless behaviour. This surprised Behaim, and he complained about how uncomfortable he felt in Verona.

"How unlike Milan this place is," he said. "Now there's a city for you! In no time at all you find good company, friends, people who appreciate you. They have the best inns, well provided with everything one could want, places where I can invite any nobleman to be my guest. There are also modest inns which are also very good, so one can spend as much or as little as one likes. And, wherever you go for a meal, they serve you with dishes of a delicacy and abundance unequalled anywhere else in the world. I know an inn where they serve you a wine which could awaken the dead. Painters and other artists frequent the place, and I was on very good terms with them."

He fell silent and thought about old times.

In Milan, after a number of exasperating experiences, he made straight for the Three Moors inn, where the best people stayed. It was here that he proposed to stay and make the acquaintance of French noblemen to whom he could sell his precious stones.

The landlord, who looked and behaved like a nobleman himself, received him politely. Behaim was satisfied with the room he was offered and the prices that were mentioned. He ordered dinner and a bedtime drink in his room, as he intended to go to bed early.

When the dishes were taken away and he had finished his

bedtime drink there was a knock at the door, and the landlord came in.

"Forgive me for troubling you, sir – I can see that you look very tired. May I ask whether you did not receive strange glances on your way here?"

"Yes," said Behaim, "and it didn't happen just once, but a hundred times, and not only here in Milan, but also in Verona, as well as in villages through which I passed."

"If I may be permitted to advise you, sir, I would suggest you cut off your beard or alter its shape. Your kind of beard is no longer worn."

"Not on your life," said Behaim, for he was proud of his well tended beard in which there was not a trace of grey hair. "People can stare at me as much as they like, I don't give a damn."

"Do as you think best, sir," said the landlord. He did not go, but added after a moment's reflection: "Have you, I wonder, visited the monks at the monastery of Santa Maria delle Grazie?"

"No. What have I to do with them?" Behaim asked in surprise.

"In their refectory there is the famous *Last Supper* by our Master Leonardo, the Florentine, which, sir, is a work that must be seen. You will certainly have met Leonardo."

"Yes," said Behaim, "I have often been in his company and, if my memory does not deceive me, he invited me to dinner or did me some other honour. Is he in Milan?"

"No, he left this city a long time ago, and he is said to be travelling," the landlord replied. "To return to his *Last Supper*, crowds have been swarming to see it for years, and not only from Milan and the whole of Lombardy, but from Venetian territory, the duchy of Mantua, the Romagna and even farther away. They come, young and old, men and women, they're even carried here on stretchers. They go to the refectory in their Sunday best as if it were a ceremonial occasion, and even the peasants come from the villages, and they too put on their Sunday best to see the *Last Supper*, and it's even said that one of them actually brought his specially decked out donkey with him. Take my advice, sir; go and have a look at it. It's something you really should do."

And with that he took his leave.

When Behaim went to the monastery refectory the next morning and stood looking at the *Last Supper* and turned his eyes from Christ and Simon Peter to Judas holding his purse in his hand, he felt as if he had received a blow in the face and his head was in a whirl.

God help me, he said to himself. Am I dreaming, or what has happened to me? What a disgraceful trick to play on me. How could he dare do such a thing?

He looked round, in the hope of finding sympathy and understanding for what had been done to him. In spite of the early hour, there were many visitors in the refectory, and they all looked at him as he stood in front of Judas. No one made a sound, the silence was as complete as it is in church when the bell rings at the Elevation. When he could face those eyes no longer and stormed out of the refectory, people at last found their tongue and began talking and calling out to one another: "Judas looking at Judas. Did you see?"

"He comes here and shows himself instead of creeping into the darkest wood or taking refuge in a desert, a cave, or some other place abandoned by the human race."

"He was attracted here like a bee to a honey-pot."

"Is he a Christian? Does he go to Mass?"

"Why should he go to Mass? God lets no seed grow in a field like that."

Meanwhile Joachim Behaim was furiously making his way back to his inn, determined not to spend another hour in Milan, and in his impotent rage he talked aloud to himself.

What a vile trick to play. Can one imagine a dirtier, more childish prank? Yet he's an old man, fit for nothing but the grave. So that's why he drew my portrait. I let myself in for it by associating with those painters and all that rabble. In heaven's name someone ought to put a stop to what this

Leonardo's doing, because how much more harm will he do if he persists in his wicked ways? A painter? He's no more a painter than a sloe shrub is a vine. He can't have much brain in that noddle of his, by the holy cross, if he couldn't find anyone better than me for his Judas. He deserves a thrashing for it, no, not just a thrashing, he ought to be a galley-slave in chains.

He had reached the cathedral square, and Simoni the woodcarver came towards him with a small boy on his left and Niccola on his right. But Joachim Behaim, with clenched fists and lowered head and rage in his heart, walked past without seeing them, swearing in the Bohemian tongue.

The woodcarver stopped and dropped the boy's hand.

"It was he," he said, with a beating heart and in a sudden cold sweat. "Did you see him?"

"Yes," Niccola replied, "I saw him."

"And . . . do you still love him?" the woodcarver wanted to know.

"How can you ask such a silly question?" Niccola replied, putting her arm round his shoulders. "Believe me, I should never have fallen in love with him if I had known he had Judas's face."

Postscript

Some readers of this book may have noticed a close resemblance between the poems I put into Mancino's mouth and those of the great French poet François Villon, who was born in Paris in 1431, studied the fine arts at Paris University from 1448 to 1452, wrote many important poems, as well as a romance in verse which takes place in the Paris students' quarter – it is unfortunately lost – and in or about 1464 disappeared so completely from the sight of his contemporaries that no one knows where he lived after 1464 or when he died.

If I admit that the verses I have put into Mancino's mouth have a distinct external and internal relationship with poems by François Villon, let it not be supposed that I am guilty of plagiarism. For in this book I have taken the liberty – perhaps it was an act of great audacity – not just to hint but to make it explicit that Mancino was none other than François Villon, student, poet, vagabond and member of a gang of thieves who, after disappearing in France, turned up again at the end of the century in Milan, where he lived his restless life among the artists who subsisted in the shadow of the Cathedral – painters, woodcarvers, bronze-founders and master-masons – and then died in an inglorious but not entirely ignoble fashion. So if he was François Villon, he has a perfect right to recite Villon's lines as his own.

Perhaps some readers will not follow me along this path, however, and will refuse to be convinced of Mancino's identity with the vanished French poet. Very well, I cannot object to a reader's taking such a line. In that case let him regard Mancino, who describes himself as a drinker, gambler, loafer, brawler and whoremonger, as a literary thief also. But whatever the reader decides, whether he takes Mancino for François Villon or for an impudent plagiarist, the epitaph that the French poet and vagabond wrote for himself and left to posterity, can apply to Mancino too. A very free translation is:

> Owned nothing, neither plate nor bowl;
> Now that his troubled life is past
> Lord, take pity on his soul,
> Grant him light and peace at last.